Existence Denied:

a search for truth and consequences

Existence Denied:

a search for truth and consequences

Mike Galley

PublishingPush

First edition 2022

Book design by Publishing Push

ISBN 978-1-80227-708-1 (paperback)
ISBN 978-1-80227-709-8 (ebook)

Typeset using Atomik ePublisher from Easypress Technologies

For Norma, my darling wife,
who loves a good read.

Chapter 1

A piercing scream of "Go!" echoed across the room.

There was silence for ten seconds, followed by a gunshot. Colin's pulse was racing, and his mind was comatose.

Alice, his wife of twenty years, murmured and fidgeted, then her slow breathing continued. It seemed she had heard nothing. He pursed his lips. *I must have been dreaming, or more like having a nightmare,* he thought. There had only been sounds, no images, just the sounds. Outside was silent; the silence, as townies would say, you can actually hear in the countryside.

Colin lowered himself back into bed, his heart thumping and his pyjamas wet with sweat. He tried to steady his breathing and still his fear because it was fear for sure. A mature grown man, one-time judo dan, scared stiff by his own internal imaginings. Colin trawled his mind for images, for any pictures to go with the sounds. There was nothing. Absolutely nothing. What should he do? Get up or try to revert to sleep?

He turned his head. The clock radio showed 3.10. He got out of bed as quietly as he could so as not to disturb his wife, Alice. She did not like to be disturbed. She usually made it known in no uncertain terms.

"I am quite capable of waking myself up," she would say sarcastically, "Thank you very much!"

What on earth had gone off in my head? Colin wondered, walking quietly across the cream carpet to the ensuite shower room.

He was awake, so he might as well have a pee, especially as he had nearly wet himself when the sounds went off.

After he had finished, he afforded himself a smile as he recalled the Cumbrian speaker at the last over-50s club meeting saying, "At our age, there are three nevers: Never pass a toilet; never trust a fart, and never waste an erection!"

That wasn't the usual fare served up by speakers. They were usually circumspect, with topics like gardens, holidays, and wines, but everybody had laughed uproariously at this.

Easing himself back into bed as quiet as a mouse, Colin sought to relax back into sleep. *Strange; no picture. Only the 'Go' and the gunshot; bloodcurdling sounds*, he thought.

He tried his usual method to block out unwanted thoughts or memories by focusing on something specific.

For some reason, Alan Raybould, an old cricketing pal, came into his mind.

Poor old Alan, he had died of cancer in his 40s. He was a great bloke and a classy batter to boot.

An ardent Leeds United fan, Alan had a fund of tales about the goings-on in the Scratching Shed at Elland Road on Saturday afternoons watching John Charles play. He had a great singing voice, and Colin recalled his performance in the *Yeomen of the Guard* held at Knaresborough Castle. Alan sang in the church choir, yet he was outrageous, totally the antithesis of Colin's public persona. Colin knew that he himself had another persona. This became most evident in his sporting activities.

Alan had a Humanist funeral, which he himself had meticulously planned.

It was the most moving spiritual experience he had ever had. A real celebration of the man and his shortened life, Colin remembered. His mind had now moved on from his nightmare. Within minutes was snoring loudly. He was unceremoniously wakened as letters dropped through the brass letter box flap onto the welcome mat, followed by the clang of the religiously polished brass inner flap.

"Bloody postman. He's deliberately noisy. He's up, so everybody else has to be," Colin muttered.

One sticky eyelid opened. The clock said 7.10, the same as every day.

Reassured his world was back in order, he heard occasional commuting cars swishing along the road outside. It was raining again.

At least once at work, he wouldn't be looking out the window wishing he was watching cricket or off sailing.

Alice, asleep or feigning it, didn't stir as he slid out of bed. Not only did she not like to get out of bed early, she didn't like to get up in one go. Anyway, she knew better to keep away from Colin in the morning. He liked his breakfast alone; well, alone in the company of Radio 4, that is.

He pushed his feet into his comfortable and somewhat worn Marks and Spencer slippers, slipped one arm into his equally ancient maroon and grey dressing gown, and pulled it on as he descended the stairs. Just one letter lay on the mat amongst the usual unsolicited junk. It was a large brown envelope. He picked it up, looked at the postmark, and saw it was marked *The Dales Building Society*, his employer.

Why are they writing to me at home, wasting money? he mused.

As usual, he almost forgot to tap in the code to switch off the burglar alarm. Was it a sign of ageing that he almost forgot so often? Was this the start? Was this how things deteriorated?

He had noticed an increasing number of times he would go somewhere and not know what he had gone for. Had Alice noticed?

Potentially worse; had his colleagues noticed?

As usual, he was just a bit surprised to see a 56-year-old facing him in the full-length mirror at the end of the hallway. Putting the mirror there had seemed a good idea when they moved into what had been his parents' home after his mother had died. She had been a widow since the war, his father having been killed without Colin ever seeing him. He grew up without the guidance of a father or a male role model. He had suffered at the hands of bullies and had taken a male teacher's advice to join a judo club. He felt driven to excel at his chosen sport.

The girls at school befriended Colin and called the bullies names. After they had all left school Mrs Allpress, the local newsagent who ran the Friday girls club, invited some boys to join in learning to dance.

The girls rejected the boys who had bullied Colin. So they got their just desserts, although Colin had to run the gauntlet at going-home time. His training included speed running, which stood him in good stead.

It had always surprised him that his mother insisted on living alone in such a big house until her end. She never remarried, which meant that Colin and Alice looked out for her and inherited the house when she died.

He still expected to see the 20-year-old he had always thought himself to be in the mirror. The telltale beginnings of lines on his face and the thinning hair gave the show away. In his mind, he was still youthful. Well, he was until he spotted the top of his head on the bank CCTV screen. Until then, he didn't know he had the beginnings of a bald patch.

"Ah well, there's a day to be got on with," Colin said aloud.

He contemplated what might be in the letter. He looked at it as he put the kettle on, measured the porridge oats into the microwave, and loaded the toaster with two slices of wholemeal seeded bread.

The kettle now boiled, Colin warmed the teapot and made the tea. Alice always insisted on china cups for tea, so they duly came out along with the skimmed milk. He frowned; that was Alice, with her decided ways, and shrugged his shoulders. Colin went through his morning exercise routine mainly geared towards muscle stretching and joint mobility. He was conscious of a developing thickness above his waist that he needed to do something about.

His breakfast ritual included deliberately not opening any letters until all was ready. This was 'clearing the decks' before action.

This deferment of pleasure was one of Colin's quirks, part of his psyche, self-denial, or cussedness. Had Alice been there, she would have sought to tease him into opening anything which might possibly be of interest to her.

"Go on, open it! Don't know how you can't bear not to," she would have said.

He poured two cups of Yorkshire tea and took one upstairs to Alice. The tea was acknowledged with a faint grunt. His wife did not admit to an awakened state, hanging on to the possibility of sleep for as long as she could. Colin retraced his steps, relieved at not having had to talk and eager to return to his Radio 4. He sipped his tea and stirred golden syrup into his porridge. Only then did he slit open the brown envelope marked 'personal and in confidence.'

What's this all about? he wondered. It was unheard of to write to him at home when he was in the office every day. He put on his specs and pulled out the document.

Then it hit him. He was gobsmacked!

This was totally out of the blue.

It must be a joke – somebody having a laugh at his expense.

Chapter 2

"What? What are they doing to me? The bastards," he hissed. They had taken him at his word without talking to him again. He hadn't meant what he had said. Somebody was getting their own back, getting him out of the way.

Colin stood up, shaking with anger. His spoon hit the floor. He stamped around the recently refitted kitchen.

They can't do that! They couldn't manage without him. Twenty years at the heart of the Dales. He *was* the Dales. His mind raced. How could he get out of it without losing face? How had it happened? You can't trust people. Someone was taking advantage of him. What could he do?

He couldn't retire.

He was too young. What would he do in retirement?

He recalled a corridor conversation with the Personnel Director, Georgina Hart, known disparagingly as Horse Ank Hart behind her not insubstantial back.

He had said that given the opportunity, he'd go like a shot, not really meaning it, just saying it as a way of expressing some minor irritation at the way things were being done by some third parties.

Colin had said it a thousand times.

It was her; she had set him up.

She.

Them. Colin was shaking with anger.

The top floor lot wanted him out. He was the old order, and they saw him as resisting change. They wanted him out as part of the strategy to modernise, drop mutuality and become a bank.

Arms locked down, fists clenched, he shouted at the top of his voice.

"The bitch, the bastards!"

Alice was down in a shot, tying her dressing gown belt and patting and straightening her hair in the full-length mirror.

"Colin, what on earth is going on? This is not like you."

He railed, waving the letter.

"Redundant; me. They are making me redundant."

"Well, that's all right then. I thought it was a matter of life and death from the noise you are making, never mind the language."

"What would I do? I can't retire. I'll fight it."

Alice scoffed.

"Fight it? You've never fought for anything in your life except in judo. You rely on me to do the fighting. You will have all the time in the world to go sailing and watch cricket. You've always said you wanted to. You can be a houseboy, and I can go full-time to art school. My tutor wants me to go full-time. He wants me to develop and exploit my talent. Going full-time, I get my MA earlier, and then we will be free to go anywhere, to do anything we want. You have always said we could manage if ever we had to."

"I've always done the right thing. I always go along with things the establishment wants. I even go along with what you or even your mother want, often against my better judgement." Colin muttered, "It's all right for you, dear." Then he shouted again.

"Houseboy? No fucking way!"

"Colin," she said sharply, "Don't use language like that in my house. I expect some art students to talk like that, but not *The Dales Building Society's* Chief Clerk. You are supposed to be a pillar of society."

"Not anymore, I'm not," he seethed. "Just watch,"

"Let me see the letter." He thrust it at her, turned his head, looking out the window but not seeing, just seething.

"I can't trust myself to say more than I might regret. I'm sorry, love; this has really got to me."

He held out his hand and hugged her.

After a little while, Alice looked over the glasses perched on her retrousse nose and said, "That's not bad; £60,000 lump sum and £20,000 a year pension and our mortgage paid up if I've read it right. We've never been so well off. And you could always get a little job if you wanted."

"I don't want a little job. I like my big job. They can't manage without me. They don't have the experience they need. I know the history there backwards. They have often said that I am essential to the Society." He reached for the Rennies. Heartburn; he had a tendency to suffer it at times of stress.

"Was, dear," said Alice quietly, back at the mirror, already thinking about being a full-time student working for her MA.

"Get your breakfast, love; get ready and get off to work. Don't leave any chinks that adversaries might take advantage of."

Chapter 3

Later that morning, Colin subconsciously walked slowly into his office garbed as usual in his grey Marks and Spencer suit, white shirt, and *Dales Building Society* grey tie with the maroon company motif together with the polished toecap black shoes, the same style as those he wore as a grammar school boy at Knaresborough all those years ago.

He wondered what the Dales' staff knew. What had they been told? Had they been told anything? On his twenty-minute drive to work, Colin had been preoccupied with the options so much he could remember nothing of the journey. He had been on autopilot. He had pondered whether he could refuse the offer.

He could challenge the terms of the offer so that they would retract on the grounds of being too expensive. He surmised he could claim constructive dismissal.

He didn't ponder the alternatives long; his pride wouldn't let him.

He thought he had spent a lifetime establishing himself as a man of his word. All the top corridor would have heard from Horse Ank that he had said he would go like a shot. Colin had never really engaged with her. He felt she resented his relationships with other senior staff. So much so that he had confided in trusted colleagues that she was more like an anti-personnel officer.

If he had to go, he would go with dignity. He would not want to lose face. Nobody must even suspect that he didn't want to go. His main problem was that those who really knew him knew that his work was his skeleton, the framework on which the flesh of his life hung.

Mavis, Colin's PA, walked into the office a few minutes later, shaking the rain from her umbrella. Slightly out of breath. Slightly late as usual with the usual excuse.

"I'm sorry, Mr Jameson, the traffic was awful again. Ripon gets worse. It's raining, so all the mums get their cars out to take the kids to school," Mavis exclaimed.

"Coffee?" she asked, hoping the offer would appease her boss. It usually did. She absentmindedly inspected her long bright red fingernails, smoothed down her tights to get rid of the wrinkles, and eased down her tight sweater. Mavis would normally do this for a male audience. She did it without realising, not flirting, but rather for approval, even acceptance. She knew her legs and figure were okay even if perhaps her secretarial abilities weren't.

This morning it was wasted on him; Colin didn't even turn round. Instead, he reached for a Rennie.

He didn't answer for a full minute, staring out of the window, not seeing the misty rain, not seeing people scurrying with heads down into the imposing entrance to the Dales' headquarters building. For once, he was not monitoring the late arrival times of those senior staff he knew were regular offenders. It was something he would never do. He was never late. He patted his jacket pocket to check that the Rennies were there. He was bound to get heartburn today, and he would surely remember this day, 15th February 1996.

"We will be having a special meeting in fifteen minutes, Mavis.

I want everybody in." Mavis was surprised. He never did anything in a hurry, never off the cuff. Something must have gone wrong. People usually came to meetings if they wanted to, ignoring Colin in effect, especially the likes of Jess.

People like her got away with murder. Mr Jameson would never confront Jess, the archetypal single mum, feminist say-it-as-it-is not to be taking liberties with.

"We'll have coffee then," intoned Colin.

"Morning. Everybody here?" He remembered what he had learned from his management course when making a speech: the ABC and the XYZ; 'Always Be Calm' and 'Check Your Zip.'

His voice felt quavery and weak, as though it belonged to somebody else.

His throat felt dry and insecure, the tenor strangely strangled as he held back the anger he felt. As he sipped his coffee, Jess walked in. Somebody whispered,

"It must be something important if she's come. She must have had a three-line whip."

There were giggles that Colin didn't appear to notice, or if he did, he pretended he didn't.

He had decided it was no time to be confronting anybody. He needed to hold himself together, keep his cool. Carry it off.

Colin cleared his throat.

"Good morning, everybody. I have some news which is both good and bad. I called this meeting because I believe you should know first, and I want you to hear it from me."

He paused, not for dramatic effect, although that was the effect. It was because he found it difficult to say the words.

"I am leaving the Society..." He tried again to clear his throat. It wouldn't clear. He sipped more coffee—shocked silence.

"Bloody hell. Where's he going? He's part of the furniture."

Everybody heard the stage whisper from Jess.

"... by mutual consent." Colin went on.

He sipped the last of his coffee, looking at his staff for a reaction over the rim of his cup. His throat was still scratchy.

"You will probably know or have guessed that I've wanted to go for some time. I have the opportunity now with the developments being planned for the Dales, of which I want absolutely no part. I am not against change. I am just not in favour of the specific changes mooted."

He continued, "I have several projects in mind; things I always wanted to do, and now I can plan to do them. I shall be leaving at the end of April. My decision. I suppose there will be the usual ritual departure event, and I'll no doubt have the opportunity to say my goodbyes and thanks then. The powers that be won't let me go without that. No doubt in due course you will be told what the arrangements are to be after my departure. So that's all, thank you."

Colin took a Rennie from the foil strip and proceeded to crunch it. Excited chatter rose as they filed out of his office.

"I bet he's being made redundant," said Jess to nobody in particular, "To make way for somebody younger, somebody who will embrace change. God knows this place needs it. What the hell will Colin do?" She scoffed, "What projects? He's lived for this place. He can't talk about anything else. He'll have the best garden and the best-decorated house in Knaresborough if I know Alice."

Alone in his office, Colin mopped his forehead. Did they believe him? He needed them to believe that he had created his own destiny. So, he had; but unwittingly, in that blasted exchange of words with Horse Ank Hart in the corridor. Perhaps the only time he had ever said something unguarded. Had she taken advantage of him through envy of his seeming to be better thought of by all and sundry, particularly Board members?

Chapter 4

It took Colin the full six weeks to the end of April of notice with the help of Mavis to sort through 20 years of accumulated paper, stuff he had hoarded, even a pair of old cricket boots and a discarded scorebook.

"I've often wondered what had happened to these." Mavis had lost count of the number of times he had said, "We might have needed it."

Even Mavis had begun to notice a sense of false bravado from Colin about his leaving. He hardly left his office. She could tell he hated the corridor conversations. He seemed to try to avoid contact with people.

"You lucky sod; I wish it were me," they would say.

So do I wish it were you, Colin thought but pretended that he couldn't wait. He would say, "There are so many things Alice and I want to get on with. There are things we have always wanted to do but never had the time. Work always got in the way. What am I going to do?"

Well, that's for me to know, he thought as he tapped the side of his nose.

Methinks he protests too much. He's beginning to believe what he's saying.

Horse Ank called him into her office and asked what he would like to be presented with at his leaving do.

"There's bound to be a big collection, you've been here so long, and you are well-liked by the staff, and indeed the Society is very generous towards its faithful servants."

Colin turned away but felt the patronising hand on his shoulder and turned to face his nemesis – the big bovine beast with the hard interior.

"Oh, a cheque will be fine, if that's all right. That is best because then I have the flexibility to spend on whatever project I pick up on first."

Colin thought it was evident that the top corridor was keeping him out of things during his notice period. Senior colleagues seemed uncomfortable in his presence, and he sensed sudden changes to the subject matter under discussion as he drew near the groups. He no longer got called in as the eminence gris he had been seen as on issues of the day.

Colin believed his strategy had worked. They thought he wanted to go. In fact, he, too, now felt as well that he wanted to go.

He was dreading the leaving ceremony. All the staff called together to listen to the Chief Executive and then the Chairman singing praises of the person leaving. So false, the poor sod had to respond and say nice things back. Colin had seen too many false rituals.

The night before the 'do,' he lay awake interminably rehearsing what he was going to say, or rather what he was not going to say. He rehearsed lashing out at the ungrateful Dales, telling them what he really thought of them. Then, of course, he knew he couldn't; he just couldn't. He would do the right thing, the expected thing. He would show no bitterness, no resentment; he would just keep up pretences.

Like he always did, he realised. Nobody would know or even suspect. But what would he say, and beyond that, what would he do in retirement?

He got through the ordeal by saying to himself that they were the losers and took home a cheque for £500; his gift from his colleagues; correction, former colleagues.

He came home, his hand wringing and his mind scrambling, with all the goodbyes and proffered good wishes and with a huge good luck card filled with signatures including many junior names he did not even know.

He said to Alice, "Well, that's it."

"That's what, dear?" said Alice absentmindedly, half preoccupied with thoughts of the seminar she had coming up the next week.

"The last day of my life."

"Correction, the last day of your working life."

She's good at corrections. Always has been, Colin silently voiced.

"You know what? I can't remember a thing about today. I spent the whole day worrying that people would see through me."

"Have you, love?" murmured his wife.

He's good at worrying, always has been. Then she said, feeling guilty for not listening to him, "Well then, tell me what happened."

Colin looked up,

"Sir Alan made a speech thanking me on behalf of the Board and handed me this." He held up an envelope.

"Inside is a cheque from Board members, which you can open if you like."

Alice quickly extracted the cheque.

"Mmm. How many Board members? Oh, there are seven signatures, and it says an amount to be added to the staff collection. The buggers. They don't want us to know how much they have given!"

"Who cares? The collection was presented by George, the finance man, on behalf of the staff. I was spared having the big woman trying to say nice things about me, and £500 was about what I thought I'd get. I responded by saying, "thank you all," and "I would treasure this.""

He held up the huge card full of signatures, good wishes, and even kisses from female colleagues.

"Don't think you can return the kisses, Colin. Don't even think about them. That's it then. It's all over. No more Dales. On with real work. God knows the house and garden need it."

Fortunately, it being May, there was plenty to do in the garden for a retired man, and this also meant Colin was not under Alice's feet. His time in the garden was in one of two modes.

His preferred mode was that of mindless maintenance: weeding, mowing, hedge cutting, or digging while listening to Radio 4.

Test Match Special couldn't come soon enough for him.

The more demanding mode was that of meeting Alice's specific instructions. Colin's maxim was 'if it ain't broke, don't fix it.' For her part, Alice was full of ideas for changes, and then she would change her mind halfway through whatever was the original idea. He wasn't sure if the changes were for improvement's sake or just to ensure he was kept busy, or perhaps that was too cynical.

There would be a discussion. The outdoor dining room was an example. Alice started with, "It needs to be moved."

"Why?" Colin asked.

"We don't use it in the evening because it's out of the sun."

"We don't use it in the evening because we like to watch the News at Six, and the sun sets in the evening anyway," Colin responded.

"We watch too much television, and you listen to the news all day long on your Walkman anyway. I'm not bothered about the news. If we move it across by about three yards, we'll get more of the evening sun. You can't deny that, dear."

"No, love, but do you realise what's involved? Every single slab has to be lifted, moved, and relaid. Two posts have to be chopped out; new holes dug, and new posts put in, and is it even worth all the effort and time?"

"I think so, and besides, you have nothing else to do, have you, dear?" Colin grunted.

"Right, that's it then." Out came Alice's standard closure line.

"We've got Greta and George coming for dinner a week on Sunday. It would be nice to have it sorted by then." Colin realised he had given in yet again.

"Oh, all right then, Alice. I'll do as you wish. I wouldn't do it for anyone else, sweetheart."

Looking in the mirror and primping her hair Alice said absently, "I think I'll have a perm before they come."

Colin reflected as he started on the slab that Alice seemed to have lost the term compromise from her vocabulary and thought processes since she became a mature student on the arts degree course. Come September, she would be a full-time student in her course. All her married life, Alice had drawn and painted. It intensified when the children left home.

She recalled that her mother had always had reservations about Colin's character. She was insightful and had warned her daughter that there was a hidden side to him.

"He toes your line too easily and too often for my liking. What is he really thinking?" she would say. Colin wondered what changes to his life would her going full-time to college bring.

Sixteen weeks later, Colin was relieved when he fastened the freshly painted wrought iron gate waving to Alice as she drove off in her red Clio to start her final year at art college as a full-time student. As he helped her load the car, he said, "You do look good for a 55-year-old."

Going to college had given her a new lease on life. She had always taken care of her appearance, almost always dressed by Marks and Spencer. Her brown hair and hazel eyes were usually complemented by autumn colours. Colin thought that since taking up with fellow students mainly in their early 20s, Alice's wardrobe had broadened. Today she had gone off in jeans, a t-shirt, and what looked like heavy boots.

Since he had left work, he had put on a stone in weight and had just about lived in cord trousers and old checked shirts. He felt he was living his age while Alice seemed to be growing younger. That's the effect of him having been thrown on the scrap heap by the Dales. To Colin, there was no longer anything to look forward to; no challenge, no young people to engage with. He lost interest in sailing and couldn't be bothered to make an effort. When he did, it was with former colleagues from the office. Even with them, it wasn't really enjoyable. They repeatedly said, "You are better off out of it the way things are."

Leaving his thoughts, he turned back to the house.

Alice had left the usual catalogue of dos and don'ts. He wondered how he would get through life when she wasn't there.

The two of them in the house together during the summer recess had been impossible. Alice couldn't wait to get away, Colin mused, but now he had some freedom. The garden was immaculate; every room in the house that needed it had been decorated.

So these were the projects for which he'd been striving to leave the Dales.

The instructions for the day's shopping were:

17

'Don't forget, only Hovis with grains. The other sorts make you constipated.'

What had things come to? A man with his skills and experience on the scrap heap.

Alice always had two modes: either hesitant, needing reassurance, or confident, pushy, and even controlling. It seemed to Colin that since he'd left work, she was more and more in the latter mode.

What was this doing to his feelings of self-worth? Even less now than they were.

Chapter 5

As he pulled down the loft ladder, Colin thought it was about time the loft was sorted. He had had neither the time nor the inclination for twenty years.

He thought that God only knew the last time Mother had got up there. Alice had said there was probably stuff up there from the war years.

Colin thought thinking about the task was probably worse than actually doing it. That's what he had found in the other jobs he had been working on.

What bugged him was the lack of value in what he was doing. At the Dales, even the most menial jobs had value; at least he was being paid.

He regularly told Alice that sixteen weeks ago, the Society was central to his life. Now it was as if it had never existed.

The ladder suddenly slid down in a rush bringing a cloud of dust. *What am I in for now?* He climbed the steps.

Where to start? The place had stuff scattered all over on top of a scanty covering of insulation foam, and there was black dust from the coal fire days of yesteryear. The old house had no roofing felt under the rosemary tiles, which had been back pointed with mortar and which was now dropping off. What a job cleaning up this lot!

One week later, he had cleared the mortar and dust, which he could even taste in his food.

Alice's words after her first day at college had been, "There's dust everywhere. I'm not stopping here. I'll move into the hall of residence until everything is sorted."

"Of course, dear, you must." He popped a Rennie into his mouth.

"Have you got indigestion, dear? It'll be the dust."

A phone call, hurried packing, and she was ready to go.

"Oh, by the way, I'll be needing to visit some galleries as part of the research for my dissertation on visual studies. New York and Santa Fe have been recommended for what I'm doing."

"Oh, yes, dear, whatever. It sounds expensive."

"Isn't it exciting? You will be able to come with me, won't you?"

Colin did not commit himself. He merely grunted.

The next day, he made his first find in the loft.

Tucked in a gap in the brickwork by a chimney stack was a biscuit tin. Inside were old letters tied in bundles and birthday cards, and a folded telegram.

His curiosity aroused, he unfolded the latter, blowing off the dust. He would find out what had happened to his dad.

The statement was bald. 'Regret to inform you 230188 Signalman J J Jameson is missing in action and presumed dead.' It was dated June 1944.

Colin frowned and sat down. After a while, he found himself sobbing.

He had never seen the telegram before. This was his first contact with his father. It took him totally by surprise. He didn't know his father had been a signalman. He wondered where and how he had died.

He descended from the loft and went downstairs. He made some coffee and stared at the words. He would find out what had happened.

A project at last!

He told Alice about his find on the phone later. She said absently, "Something different for you to do, dear."

The reply to his letter to the Central Registry Service record centre said simply that he must be mistaken. Army number 230188 had a different name assigned, and that named soldier had survived the war.

His second approach had been to the Ministry of Defence. The reply was equally disappointing and intriguing; there was no record of J J Jameson having been in the Royal Signals in 1944.

Colin felt that was the end of the project. He was up against a brick wall. But what had his father been up to? He had been a soldier. Colin could vaguely remember a photograph of him in uniform. Photographs? There must be some in the loft somewhere.

He resumed his search.

Two days later came the second find. In a torn and grubby stamp collection was a triangular scrap of an envelope. Part of the postmark was evident *que, ico*, and what looked like *e 1944*. That part of the address looked to have been written by a child. Colin wondered who. He pondered over the postmark while watching television that night. He got out an atlas, but although he scanned place names in every European country until late in the night, he found nothing to identify it.

At the weekend, he shared his second find with Alice.

"Mmm," the not-very interested Alice then came strongly about wanting to clinch the trip to the States.

"It is not as if we can't afford it. It's not as if you can't go now you are not working. All that will stop us is your attitude. You don't have to trail around galleries if you don't want to. Just come with me; drive me around; plan your own itinerary; do your own thing." Colin said, "All right then. I'll think about it. I'll get some ideas from the travel agent as well as costs. When will you want to go? Presumably, it will have to be in the college holidays?"

"Not necessarily. We could go at half-term and take an extra week as we used to when the kids were at school."

"And where is it you want to go, precisely?"

"New York and Santa Fe."

"Santa Fe? What's it got to do with art?"

"Santa Fe is the art centre of the USA."

"Right, that's it then." The standard closure from Alice. *I've given in again.*

Colin popped a Rennie in his mouth.

"Heartburn again, Colin," said Alice.

The phone rang. The travel agent spoke as though he had better things to do.

"You do realise, Mr Jameson, that you can't fly to Santa Fe."

Colin didn't know whether to be glad at this complication which might possibly kill off the trip, or to be angry with the big shot on the phone.

"Oh, well, where can I fly to that is somewhere near?" Colin grunted.

"I'm not sure. I'll have to look at the tables."

"Well, please do. Presumably, we could drive from somewhere near enough."

The realisation hit him a few days later, as soon as he opened the itinerary sent to him by the travel agent. Fly Manchester to Newark, New York; Newark, then New York to Albuquerque, New Mexico.

The scrap of the envelope! Albuquerque, New Mexico, e 12 64

Only one month ends in 'e'- June! So it was 12 June 1964.

That evening he phoned Alice excitedly.

"Got a pen and paper? Write down underneath each other Albuquerque and New Mexico. Now underline the last three letters of each. Right, now write underneath 'e 12 64.' Recognise it? Que, ico. and June 1964."

"What are you babbling on about, Colin?" Alice said impatiently.

"You know the stamps on the scrap of the envelope I found in the loft I showed you?"

"Oh yes, that's clever. How did you work that out?"

"I just did, that's all."

Chapter 6

The holiday was booked: departure date, 20 October.

Colin resumed 'operation loft' and received a third jolt from the past.

He was clearing the last corner of the loft where the roof came down low, so low that he had to lie down to reach what appeared to be largely discards of sketches for paintings.

Alice had done this in the 1960s when she first became interested in art. Her passion had certainly developed, and she persevered. The corner seemed to have been a dumping ground for discards of Alice's works from that time.

"Don't throw anything of mine away," Alice had said.

Dare I throw anything away, he wondered.

She would probably laugh at me.

The old leather bag seemed full of jottings, notes from art trips, and earlier art courses. He separated what looked like rubbish for Alice to decide what to discard. Really, he just wanted to ditch them.

An envelope slid out from between some A4 typewritten sheets.

The writing on the envelope was adult. It was addressed to Mrs A. Jameson and sported a return zip code 87125; obviously, a US postmark. Colin went downstairs and phoned the Post Office, which told him it was a New Mexico code.

A pity the date's obscured, he mused. He went back into the loft. There was a letter, a love letter. There was no mistaking it.

It began, 'Hi, babe.' He read on, his curiosity aroused.

It was signed, 'I will always love you, Chuck.' A string of kisses followed it.

Colin felt sick. He shook angrily, clambered down the ladder, and went downstairs like an automaton. He made coffee, eventually got a hold of himself, and re-read the letter properly without the red mist.

Colin thought of Alice, his staid, conservative Alice with a lover! She was no more likely than him to have a lover, but here was evidence. He felt a surge of heartburn and reached for a Rennie.

It seemed it was a letter written by an American airman who had earlier been stationed in England. He had written when he was back in the US at a base near to where he had been brought up. Judging by the contents, Alice and whomever Chuck was, had been more than just good friends. Colin tried to think.

When did she meet this Yank? Was there any clue in the letter?

How could she? He was interested in art. That'll be it. They probably met on some arty-farty society visit to a gallery. Colin never went; they never interested him.

What should he do? Confront her? Then what?

Santa Fe was in New Mexico.

Was Chuck why Santa Fe had become a desirable destination for Alice? The letter was old and undated, written in ink with the sending address obliterated, perhaps censored. The envelope was addressed to 'Mrs,' so she was a married woman when the letter was sent.

Only recently had letters been arriving before he left for work. Hitherto, letters in rural Yorkshire came after he had left for work. The letter smacked of illicitness, not outpourings of love but little intimacies like 'we both had our hands full,' which made him want to scream; made him feel impotent.

What could he do? What should he do? The mid-60s was when he was at night school in Leeds chasing qualifications while she was chasing a good time with a Yank. What was it?

Overpaid, oversexed, and over here. He never picked up even a hint. The bitch two-timed him, and he never knew until now…

Heartburn again. He chewed on a Rennie. *I need to get some more.* It occurred to him absently. His mind was full.

After a while of contemplation, he moved on.

It was perhaps best to do nothing, say nothing. It was 30 years ago. He decided to do nothing for now but would try to find something about Chuck when they got to Santa Fe. He knew there were air bases in New Mexico.

Suddenly he was more secure, more his own man for the first time since redundancy. A man with a purpose again.

He liked the notion of knowing, and Alice not knowing, that he knew what he knew. He would spend his time in New York trying how to find out how to catch up with his 'old buddy Chuck,' who had been based in the UK, probably at Manston.

Colin found himself looking at his wife a lot when she was at home; perhaps observing her would be a better description.

He wondered how it started, how far she went. It had taken years of patient courting to even get to first base.

Several times she caught him looking at her.

"Why are you looking at me like that?"

"I didn't realise I was. Can't a man look at his wife?"

"You sort of look at me, or through me; more, more…" Alice grasped for a word, "More like me when I look at a model when I'm drawing. It's not altogether nice being looked at like that by your husband. It's like being inspected. It's not a caring look."

"I sometimes wonder if you still love me," Colin grunted.

"Course I do." But she appeared to be preoccupied with something. Alice had never given any hint that she had ever taken up with any other man.

He remembered once confiding to a colleague in an alcohol-affected conversation whilst on a management course, precisely just that.

Chapter 7

The packing was done. The police had been notified that the house would be unoccupied with the burglar alarm switched on. The next-door neighbour, Maureen Day, had a key and knew the alarm code.

Whether she would be able to remember it if it came to it was another question. She could be such a drip, but she was near and willing and available.

They drove to Gatwick Airport in Alice's red Clio. The conversation was desultory. Alice kept her excitement in check while Colin focused on the motorways' traffic or listened to Radio 4. Alice vouchsafed that their children were showing no signs of producing grandchildren for them.

Colin merely inclined his head. When they had parked up, Colin began to moan.

"Look at these impossible queues: dreary security procedures; bleary-eyed passengers humping cases and pushing trolleys moving seemingly at random and settling into complicated queues, herded like cattle. I hate flying."

"Too late now, Colin, love. Grin and bear it."

The flight seemed to take forever. The plane was full, and the movie was full of violence and F words, but they stepped out into the humidity of a warm New York October day eight hours later. The man at the information desk said the bus service was faster and cheaper than a taxi. Faster because there were bus-only lanes and a take-on/drop-off service to individual Manhattan hotels. So they took the bus. Alice's obvious excitement was equally and oppositely matched by Colin's moroseness, while she mentally buzzed like New York itself.

"Look at that! Did you see that? Did you see that skyscraper? Look, there's another. Did you ever see such traffic, so many people rushing about? Where are they all going? Isn't it exciting?" Colin just grunted.

"How much do I tip the driver?"

"Noise is going to be a problem, and unless there's good sound-proofing, I'll not sleep with all that hooting and police sirens wailing."

They stepped out onto 54th Street and into the Grosvenor hotel. A flunky took their bags, and Colin had a tip issue again.

"I don't think the boy was impressed!"

"Bellhop." She corrected him. "Not boy."

Once in the room, having booked in, Alice turned on the air conditioning, saying its constant noise would be more sleep-inducing than the outside noise. The lights flashing from the all-night girlie show across the street would be a bigger nuisance, she thought, although the flight spectacle covers would be useful.

After a hotel snack of chicken on rye and coffee, Colin braved walking out onto Broadway with Alice at her insistence. Adrenalin would keep her awake.

"I love it! Isn't it great?"

"Huh. Just be careful when we cross the road. There's no jaywalking. Don't just rely on me; you will be out on your own most of the time trailing around galleries. Remember, it's first look left over here."

"I'm grown up, Colin. I know how to cross roads. You should come with me. It's a once-in-a-lifetime opportunity to see great art, classical and contemporary."

Another grunt from Colin.

"You can be a boring old fart. What will tomorrow bring for me? You can do whatever you want, if anything," was Alice's response.

The next morning they ate bagels with a schmear of cream cheese and drank coffee from cardboard cups on a pavement cafe. Then they strolled along the eastern side of Central Park with crowds walking rapidly to work in the opposite direction.

They went past the Whitney and made for the Guggenheim gallery. Here Colin left Alice to gravitate through both and then go on to the Museum of Modern Art on a street parallel to 54th Street.

"See you back at the hotel about six-ish." That gave him the whole day to start on his project.

"What will you do?" asked Alice.

"Oh, don't worry about me. There's plenty of things I want to see and do."

"Like what? Don't go anywhere I might want to see." But Colin had gone.

His first stop was the library on Eighth Avenue. The swarthy-faced and hyper-bright young man behind the lime green large spec frames was very helpful or was trying to give the impression that he was trying to help if he could.

Colin asked, "How do I go about trying to trace an ex-GI from the 60s called Chuck?"

The young man told him he was not even at first base.

"All you have is the first name, which might even be a nickname. No date, no number, no surname. I can't see any point in continuing unless you can come up with at least a surname. With a name and number, you could try Army records in DC. I'll get you the number just in case."

The obvious futility dawned on Colin.

He realised he was a prat. A grade A pillock even to think he could get anywhere with what he had. Nonetheless, when he came across the Army recruitment centre in Times Square, he couldn't resist going in and asking. He went past the fresh-faced youngster at the desk and walked up to a tough-looking older Master Sergeant.

That was his mistake. That was evident in the man's immediate demeanour. It became manifest as soon as Colin asked his question. The old soldier looked around, either to ensure he had an audience or to ensure there was nobody who mattered within earshot.

"Respectfully, sir, this is a recruitment centre for the US Army, not a Missing Persons Bureau. And anyway, not even the FBI and CIA together and Scotland Yard could find your man with what you've got. With respect and to be frank and trying not to offend, sir, what you've got is so old and so remote," he said heavily.

"Go figure ... You ain't got shit!"

Red-faced, Colin left hurriedly and sought refuge in a nearby bar, where he spent a long time staring into a Budweiser. He concluded he should forget it and find something to enjoy from this over-expensive trip. Forget the wild goose chase.

So what if his wife had been entertaining a far-from-home Yank 30 years ago? He hadn't known, so what had it done to him?

Nothing. And she had decided to stay with him. He wondered who had made the first move. He felt anger rising.

Alice rarely, if ever, made the first move with him. He squirmed; he was torturing himself. He walked back to the hotel to await her. Presumably, she would be shattered and only want to write notes on what she had seen, then eat and go to bed.

Colin found himself outside the girlie 24-hour show. He paused outside, but as the doorman started to open the door, he lurched off muttering to himself what a wimp he was, nearly knocking over two diminutive Japanese who clearly were not wimps as they made their way out laughing.

"Who won the war any-bloody way!" he shouted unreasonably, although it did make him feel a bit better.

He dozed on his hotel bed until Alice arrived. Of course, she had a wonderful time.

"You should have seen..." was repeated ad infinitum.

"Where are you going tomorrow? I thought I might come with you," Colin said matter of factly, looking at a street map of Manhattan.

"Never mind tomorrow, let's get out and eat and get a shot of New York after dark." They joined the raucous fast-moving nighttime bustle that is New York and strolled the streets full of light and noise and thronged with people.

Later, as Alice was getting into bed and poking plugs in her ears and donning the eye mask, she said, "Tomorrow I need to go to the contemporary gallery in Soho and as many of the commercial galleries as I can."

"I'll come with you. I suppose if I get fed up, I can always have a ride on the Staten Island ferry and take a photo of the Statue of Liberty."

"Suit yourself," she grunted. Touche!

In a bookshop in Soho, Colin picked up a tourist guidebook, 'In and Around Santa Fe.' There he would need to hire a car to get around. A car would have been a waste in New York.

He realised he had not had indigestion since the start of the trip and wondered why. He was out of Rennies but knew in the US that Tums were the equivalent.

They took the bus to Newark Airport. Checking in for the American Airlines flight to Albuquerque seemed casual by UK security standards. As take-off time approached, a Middle Eastern man got up and left the plane.

A British ex-pat across the aisle from Colin said to the steward, "Hey, has that man got off the plane?"

"He sure has. He forgot something."

"Is he coming back?"

"No, sir."

"Then where is his bag? He got on with one."

"I dunno, sir. I'll check."

"You're bloody right you will."

A few minutes later, the laconic voice of the pilot announced there would be a short delay. The plane had missed its take-off slot on account of a problem related to a passenger.

The passenger had gotten off the plane, leaving his bag with his wife and child still on board. The vigilant Brit said, "You can't let these things go; you never know." Despite the flight delay, the Brit was regarded as a hero, especially by the couple alongside him.

"You a Brit? I was in the US Army in Cambridge during the war. Where are you from, or where were you from? Yorkshire, you say. We love that Princess Di. Some folks think she shouldn't have taken up with the royals."

Colin stayed quiet.

The flight was uneventful, with the pilot spending most of the time chatting with passengers. He was casually dressed, very relaxed, too relaxed for some.

The Jamesons picked up the rental car but not before Colin had been induced into paying extra for an upmarket model by a smooth-talking and personable young woman.

"Anything in a skirt could sell you anything," sniffed Alice. Colin bit his tongue but thought that he hadn't bought anything like what she had bought in the 60s. When he found Chuck, he'd show him a few judo throws.

They drove the turquoise route to Santa Fe, stopping off at Madrid, now an artists' village, to look at some artefacts.

The artists had moved into the village 30 years earlier when the coal mines closed and the miners left. Ghost Town Madrid was hot, dry, and dusty, although a cute place immortalised in Wild Hogs, which Alice recalled and related to Colin from some forgotten past.

They had coffee at Mamma Lisa's at what was claimed to be the longest bar in the state, where they were told they shouldn't miss the old mine museum. That was good information. They saw a real coal seam and rang the bell on the 1900s steam loco. They went back to the bar for lunch and were again steered, this time to the glass showrooms and particularly to the work of glass artist Jezebel.

They continued their drive after Colin had managed eventually to drag Alice away. They found a motel on Cerrillo Road just outside Santa Fe. They went out to eat hot Mexican food washed down with large Margaritas in a restaurant sited at the old railroad station. They slept well.

Chapter 8

The next morning, Colin dropped off Alice at the Georgia O'Keefe museum in Santa Fe and set off to see the experimental museum at Los Alamos, which he had read about in the guidebook he had bought in New York.

Colin had picked up that this was the city-that-never-was; the secret location where the Allies had developed the atomic bomb, which was eventually to end the Second World War.

He told Alice that he had always been interested in anything to do with the war and reckoned she wouldn't be at all interested.

Colin almost drove past the Centre for Research. He found the right road but struggled to get the right direction. He reckoned it would be a regular navigation problem for him. To Colin, they listed the destinations in the wrong order. He was mesmerised by the panoramic mountain views and exhilarated by the winding drive on open roads.

When he reached his destination, he paid the concession rate available to over-50s for entry to the centre and started the tour.

A tannoy announcement said there would be a video presentation on the history of the development of the atomic bomb in 15 minutes in the lecture auditorium on the second level. The presentation would last 18 minutes, and there would be no admissions after it had started.

Colin watched a demonstration of static electricity by a pimply youth with braces on his teeth who struggled to get the largely non-technical audience surrounding his demonstration to understand what he was saying. They were there solely for the video.

Spraying saliva droplets over those nearest to him, he asked for a volunteer to help him. A young woman wearing a tight-fitting blouse of light material and holding a child with long blonde hair took pity on him and stepped forward.

"Watch the effect on this child's hair (saliva sprayed everywhere) when I bring up this rod which, as you saw, I stroked with a piece of silk."

Sure enough, the hair of the child rose as he approached with the rod, but what was of more interest to the male half of the audience was the effect on the girl's blouse. Or, to be precise, on what was under the blouse.

"Jesus, just lookya at the nipples on them titties. They are like chapel hat pegs. Bertha, I sure need to get o' them, that-there rods," an elderly American laughed.

"Shush! Hush your mouth, Harold. You'll get us thrown out."

Everyone else laughed except the girl, who blushed, perhaps as much with pride as with embarrassment.

Colin was impressed. He was betting the lad would want to repeat that experiment!

The video presentation started. It made plain the intense secrecy surrounding the setting up of the research centre. A former Scouts' adventure camp, it was taken over by the US Government as Winston Churchill met President Roosevelt to set up arrangements to attempt to beat Hitler to develop the atomic bomb at all costs. Top European and American scientists and technologists were gathered with all the facilities they needed under absolute secrecy and security.

Colin thought the video was like an old Movietone news, except that it had never been allowed to be news. He had never previously heard of just how the harnessing of atomic power had been approached. He watched, fascinated at shots of men and women in civilian clothing arriving at the Santa Fe railway station and being documented. Suddenly he leapt to his feet.

"That's my Dad," he yelled. He sat down embarrassed, muttering, "It is; I know it is." He was absolutely staggered. He knew he must be wrong. His father was not a scientist. He was in the Royal Signals, just a signalman.

Then it happened again. There were shots of a dance or a party, and this fresh face looked directly at the camera and held his frank gaze long enough for Colin to know he was not wrong.

"It was him. It is my father," he harked back to the wedding photo. "Yes!"

Suddenly he realised that the woman who had introduced the video was asking questions. She said, "This was one of the turning points in history. The tremendous efforts of the people assigned to the Manhattan Project were working under extreme pressure at the limits of man's knowledge taking risks to bring about something to shorten the duration of the war. In fact, it shortened the war by some two years. It did result in thousands of Japanese lives being lost but probably saved many more Allied lives."

There were a couple of questions, and then Colin asked, "Please can you tell me when I can see the video again," thinking he would have to return the next day.

"We only show the video twice a day, and I am afraid you have seen the second and last of the day, sir. The museum shop on the way out may have a copy, although I doubt it. There is an excellent book which tells the whole story of the atomic research not only here but elsewhere too."

The museum shop had no videos.

"I don't suppose you could make a copy?" He knew straightaway his negatively phrased question would invite a negative response. And it did. He turned to walk away and then turned back.

"Do you know how to make a copy? Do you have the kit to make a copy?"

"Well, yes and yes, but I am not allowed. I am a non-technical staff, so…"

"What will it cost me? It is vitally important that I get a copy. I've come all the way from the UK. It's actually a life and death issue." Little did Colin know how prophetic his statement would prove. He pulled out his pocketbook. The youth shook his head.

"I can be either generous or violent. Which do you want?" growled

Colin, continuing, "I was British judo champion. Go figure, as you Yanks would say."

This was true, but not many people knew. 'Judo is not to be used or threatened' was his teacher's tenet. The shop boy responded conspiratorially.

"Actually, it's on a DVD which the techie will copy for $50 cash."

"Good lad. I'll be in the coffee shop. Let me have that book to be looking at."

Just after three thirty and two refill coffees later, Colin handed over the money and put the brown envelope in his pocket, and strode off to the car parking lot, delighted with himself and his find.

I thought I had come to New Mexico to look for Chuck; instead, I've found my father, or at least where he had spent the war.

Colin recalled the saying, 'If you come to a fork, take it.' Well, to quote the vernacular, he sure would.

He drove back to Cerrillo Road as fast as he dared to find the 55 mph speed limit irksome on the open roads. He spotted a brown sedan coming toward him. It was a police car with the driver motioning him to pull in. He did so.

"Stay in the car with your hands where I can see them. Okay, passport, please. Ah, a Brit. You don't have head-on speed guns. We do. You were doing 65. I'll make you out a speed ticket. Get caught again, and it will be jail. On your way, Mister, and at the lawful speed."

Colin was a pitiful apologist, albeit relieved. He hadn't gone far when he realised he had got his direction wrong and had to make a U-turn.

En route, he wondered why his father was reported missing, presumed killed, and thought to be in Europe.

He couldn't wait to see the DVD and show Alice.

When he got to the motel, he saw Alice had gotten there before him and thought she would be swimming. He fished out his speedos and a towel and hurried to the pool. She was in one of the two jacuzzis with a huge older man.

"Hello," she said and then hurriedly, "The other's not working, so we are sharing this one. This is my husband, Colin. Love, this is Sam."

"Hi, Sam, good to meet you. Alice, I've made the most fantastic discovery. You know I always believed my father was missing and presumed dead in Europe in the war. Well, he couldn't have been. He was at the Los Alamos atomic research centre where they invented the atomic bomb for use against the Japs at Hiroshima."

"Really?" Alice replied. "I thought that was where John Wayne fought the Mexicans."

"No, that was the Alamo, not Los Alamos."

"Now that was another Texan," said the man, "I think I'll go white water rafting tomorrow. You guys want to come along?"

"I'd love to, but Colin won't. In any case, I've got a full day organised for tomorrow. We're only here for a short time."

Colin said, "I might need to be here a bit longer. I'm determined to find out what happened to my father."

"That was 50 years ago," said Alice pulling a face at the Texan.

"What's the point?" meaning there wasn't any point. "Because I don't see it."

"Come on, love, let's go. I've got a DVD to show you. You will be amazed."

Alice feigned interest but was sceptical about Colin's identification of the man in the film. She was unhappy at the notion of Colin staying longer. She couldn't stay even if she wanted to; she had to get back on course at college.

"Look, you have seen the face on the DVD. That is my father; of that, I have no doubt. I simply have to find out more; I just have to, and this is my only chance to find out what happened to him. The authorities in the UK said he didn't exist. We have a telegram that says he was missing and presumed killed. I owe it to him and myself to bottom this and find out the truth if I can. I am absolutely determined to do it."

Alice nodded, thinking that she had not seen Colin as positive as this since the one time she saw him on the judo mat in the British final. Perhaps this is the side of him her Mum alluded to.

"I'll take you to Albuquerque airport and see you onto the plane. You need only take a small bag, and you can pick up the car at Gatwick. It's a piece of cake." Alice's sniff spoke volumes, but she knew that was it.

"I still don't see the need for you to stay on here. You can use technology to do most anything these days. Still, if you are so determined, you had better get it out of your system. I'll get back to college and write up my findings from the New Mexico art world. As we have only two days left, I'll spend the time with you once we've sorted out my flight change."

They visited a church to see contemporary body paintings by a female artist working in Santa Fe; some of them were a bit too risque for Colin to be in a church. They drove out to the Bandolier monument, the former home of the Hopi Indians. Both were fascinated. They climbed ladders to get into a cave in the rock face said to have been used for ceremonials.

A young woman was already there taking photos. "Can we do a swap?" asked Alice. "I'll take a photo of you if you take a photo of us."

"Yes, for sure," said a strong, clear voice pitched low, somewhere mid-Atlantic.

Photos shot, the threesome set off together through the trees to the monument reception centre. Alice engaged the woman in conversation.

The newfound acquaintance had light coffee-coloured skin with jet black hair and was dressed in a white shirt and black pants. She was clearly ready for the office. Colin noticed she was well-spoken, educated, and quite beautiful. She told Alice she was interested in art and artefacts and was working in the DA's office in the State Capitol in Santa Fe.

She had some spare time on a case and so was playing at being a tourist. She told Alice that the State Capitol was well worth a visit to see the contemporary and Native American art there. Most people missed it, which was a shame. This was corporate buying of the best of both worlds and was set in beautiful surroundings.

The next morning Colin went with Alice up and down Canyon

Road, the epicentre of art and artists working in Santa Fe. They went to every gallery and workshop. It was hot. Alice could not bypass anything and drank in every line and every shade of colour while conversing with many of the artists and gallery owners.

Chapter 9

Eventually, they arrived back at the motel with a take-out. They packed Alice's things for her return flight the next day and collapsed into bed. The next day, by 9 a.m., they were at Albuquerque airport. Not once did they take the wrong direction. A good omen? They breakfasted on huevos rancheros which cheered Alice up no end, rating it as her best-ever breakfast, if not meal, full stop. She reminded Colin to phone at the right time of day for the UK. She made it clear she didn't want to be woken up at all hours.

They waved to each other as she climbed into the Air America plane to Dallas Fort Worth en route to the UK. Colin spotted Tums in the airport shop and picked up a pack, just in case.

He wondered what to do next and felt elated at being free to pursue any whim without hindrance or feelings of guilt for a whole week. But what would the week bring?

Colin went directly back to the dreary motel room with its faded drapes, finger-marked light switches, and grimy wallpaper. He took out the book *the city that never was,* which he had taken from the coffee house at the museum. He had forgotten to give it back, and the youth had not asked. He knew that wasn't like him. Of course, he would send it back when he had read it. Perhaps!

These things he mused over as he walked the two blocks into downtown Santa Fe. He sat down in a noisy, smoky bar and ate a massive steak and fries, and started watching a baseball game on TV, which was competing with a guitarist trying to get his music across to a largely disinterested audience.

Walking back to the motel, he passed a respectable bar that backed onto a hotel when a woman stepped out and said cheerfully and slightly drunkenly, "Come on in; don't go past. You must be foreign, walking when you could ride. Come in. The piano player is great."

Out of character and perhaps because he was preoccupied, Colin walked in.

"You don't have to eat, and the coffee is great, and refills are free," she intoned. Colin sat at a table near the woman and ordered coffee. The piano player was on his break and was at the bar laughing and joking with men in cowboy garb.

The woman walked over to the bar and said loudly, "I know it's your break, but get playing, or the Brit I brought in will think I gave him a bum steer." The man looked up and then turned back to his conversation.

"He won't be long. In the meantime, meet Milly."

She fished in her bag and produced a small turquoise shell.

"My brother gave it to me today. We used to catch hermit crabs when we were kids." Colin thought she was decidedly both strange and the worse for wear.

"Look," she said, holding out her hand when the shell dropped to the floor.

"Oops! I'll just poke her back in. She'll be all right." She pushed the crab back into the shell.

"It's real," said the astonished Colin.

"Of course it is. I ain't no tall-storyteller."

The piano player got up and started to play *A Nightingale Sang in Berkeley Square*. Then a cowboy got up and sang along. Colin felt trapped. This was for his benefit, so he felt he couldn't leave. Then a couple strolled in from alongside the restaurant. They were deep in conversation. They sat on bar stools and ordered coffee. Colin recognised her as the woman he and Alice had met at the Bandolier Monument two days earlier. He couldn't have mistaken her.

The song had finished. The performers were looking at him. He clapped perhaps a little too enthusiastically. The couple at the bar turned to look who was making the noise. They turned back in animated conversation, and Colin walked to the bar and said to the barman, pointing to the musician, "Whatever they are having. Use the card." He then handed it over to him.

Colin was disappointed that the woman hadn't recognised him. Sniffing, he ordered a brandy and went back to the crab woman and listened to more songs.

The woman was showing the crab to other customers, who were polite but exchanged knowing looks. The couple came over to see what the fuss was. As they left the table, the beautiful lady turned to Colin, "Don't I know you?"

"Bandolier Monument. Wasn't it great?"

"Actually, there's something I'd like to ask you." Surprised at his temerity, perhaps it was the drink. Colin shuffled his feet nervously. She replied, "Yes, I know, you want to see the photos I took, and me yours. Where is your wife? Alice, wasn't it?" Colin nodded and decided it was better not to say that Alice had gone home.

"I'm on the second level. Ask for Elvira at reception."

"Thanks, I'll not forget that." Acknowledging the band and saying goodbye to the crab woman, he took the opportunity to walk out onto the street.

It was exactly 10 a.m. the next day as Colin got to the desk in reception on the ground floor of the very impressive Santa Fe rotunda.

I bet everybody who works here gets a buzz every time they walk in, and the taxpayers wince every time they look at it, he thought.

"Walk on up," was the response when he said he had an appointment with Elvira. He tapped on the door with her name on it, and a voice said, "Yes, oh, you are on time. No wife again?" looking over his shoulder.

"Yes, well, I didn't get the chance to explain. Alice had to return home. In fact, to tell the truth, I'm not really interested in art."

"You had better explain yourself," she said mockingly, head cocked to one side.

Gosh, she is beautiful, Colin thought. Even in office garb, she looked a million dollars. "To tell the truth, I'm here on another matter, if you can spare me a minute, please."

"It all depends on what the matter is rather more than anything else. We will have some coffee." She said to her PA, "Get Mr…?"

"Colin, er Colin Jameson is my name."

"Right. Some coffee." was the drawn-out response.

"Where shall I start, er?" Colin paused, frowning.

"The clock is ticking," said Elvira.

"We always believed my father had been killed in the war 50 odd years ago. We had a telegram saying as much, and we had every reason to believe that it was in the European theatre of war. Then we come on holiday to Santa Fe, and I visit Los Alamos. That's where I see my father in a video which shows he was here in 1943."

"Mistaken identity. It happens all the time. It's a helluva long time ago."

Colin wondered: Was that a statement or another challenge?

"No!" Colin's shouted response shocked him, although he knew he was capable of going over the top when thwarted. This alacrity served him well in judo contests and when he needed to show he meant business.

"Okay, okay. go on."

"I've looked at the film scores of times, and I am absolutely in no doubt. It's him."

"How old were you when you last saw him?"

"I never saw him, only pictures. Well, one picture, really. There are two shots on the DVD."

"Two more shots than you've had." Colin felt his temperature rising.

"I might as well go now if you don't believe me."

"No, it's just beginning to get interesting. You'd make a good and credible witness. Credibility is more important than evidence sometimes. Drink your coffee. What do you think you want from me and that I may be able to help with?"

"Well, it's clear to me that I need to pursue with the military records people in both the US and the UK the fact…" Colin paused momentarily and got a nod to go on.

"The fact that my father was employed by both powers in the development of the atomic bomb at Los Alamos."

"When we have established that fact," she stressed the word '*we*,' "Then we can pursue the circumstances of his death or disappearance." He nodded.

"You said *we*."

"Yes, I did, didn't I? The truth is that I have a gut feeling; no, an omen or two. The name on my door says Collins; that's close to your name, Colin."

"Secondly, my father left my sister and me when I was two, so I never really knew him, and I still have doubts about his life."

"Thirdly, I took to Alice when I met her, and fourthly, I am a sucker for causes.

So, all in all, I'd like to help, but I can't promise anything, and I can't do anything in my official capacity. But I just love to solve mysteries!"

"If I am going to try to help you, I suggest we need a blind. Why don't we make out to third parties that this is a family thing? So, okay if I refer to you as Uncle? Is Uncle Colin okay?"

"Anything you say, thanks. I'd have preferred cousin." He faded; she laughed.

"So, I have a week left here. Where do I start?"

"Well, the research centre is no longer a military establishment, so I don't see much point in looking there. You are going to have to get into contact with whatever agency looks after records of military personnel, probably at the Pentagon. You need a contact there, preferably someone whom you can get to be sympathetic to your cause rather than official channels. We might have to use camouflage again as you did with me. You know, get in on one pretext in order to get at the other."

She paused and thought for a moment. Colin gazed into her eyes, beautiful brown eyes. He jerked back to reality as she said, "Mmm, you'll need someone like a British expat working in the records set up or someone who is married to an expat. You will probably have to give the impression that you are looking for something a little more recent than 1943, although you could hit on someone who has a special interest in the city-that-never-was. I wonder if there is anything like an old employees association in New Mexico? That's something I can pursue here. You have a shot at the Pentagon, and we'll meet for dinner perhaps and compare notes."

"Okay, where? How about the crab-lady place?"

"No way, that's too, well, not noisy, but we won't get left to ourselves. I'll meet you at Rosantos at eightish. It's on Cerillo."

"That's across from my motel. Great."

"Now scoot. I have a real job to do." She waved him away dismissively, and Colin left mightily impressed at the professional and direct approach of the woman. He thought nothing would faze her, and it was incredible that she had volunteered to help. He felt he owed his wife for being like her to such an extent.

Colin was halfway through his second Margarita when Elvira walked into Rosantos very, very late.

"I had almost given you up but am delighted you have made it."

"Sorry, when the boss calls, I have to be there for him. Sometimes I think he's either just trying to make me or demonstrating some power thing. I prefer older men; they have maturity."

"Oh, I have plenty of that," laughed Colin, "Let's order before I get too tipsy to talk sense."

"So where have we got to then, Uncle?" she said teasingly as she handed her jacket to the waiter.

"Well, nowhere really. There is an archives place in Washington DC. I got the number, well, several numbers. All I have learned is that records were released under the 50-year rule, which I already knew."

"Those records are held in the archive library and are accessible to permitted persons. The bad news is that I am probably not a permitted person because I am not a US citizen, and in any case, the records are believed not to include any records of foreign nationals and… I may not be able to access them even if there are records without express permission from the UK government. Seeing that the UK War Office has already informed me that they have no record of my father in their archives, I have to say that I have drawn a blank."

"Oh dear, you seem remarkably laid back about it, or are you just being very British about it? Very stiff upper lip? Here's the food. Chicken salad a la mode; it's a good choice. Cold food usually means no waiting so let's eat."

"Okay." She gave Colin that penetrating look, that eye-before -the verbal challenge he knew would follow.

"Go on, tell me what you really think."

Colin hesitated, breathed in deeply, and against all his upbringing, hissed to the lady just what he thought.

He said, "I am frustrated, really, really frustrated. It is as though the world and his mate are putting up every possible obstacle."

"And how do you feel about that?"

"It makes me the more determined." He was so loud that people turned to look.

"Good, so we don't quit yet," she laughed.

Elvira had done a bit better. She had actually made it to the research centre when a witness she was due to see didn't show. She had asked if there were any known former employees or people who might recall the names of staff who were there during the war years. It wouldn't be easy because people were brought together from all over the US and Europe to work on a project of the highest secrecy known as the Manhattan Project, and then were largely disbanded. Even so, there were some leads. Some people stayed put to work for the centre in its post-war role after the research was completed.

Elvira said, "If some of those were, say, aged from 25 to 60 in 1943, they would be over 70 now. Right? And at 70-plus, where are they likely to be living?"

"Seeing that the snowbirds flock to the southwest to live, at least in the winter, you might expect to find some in care homes for the elderly. Right, Uncle?"

If she's not triumphant, she is defiant, he thought.

"And," Elvira went on again, "I managed to get my PA to obtain a list of care homes in and around Santa Fe. Not a lot of places, but distances might seem a bit long."

"How many?" Colin asked.

"Seventeen. Have you got a map?"

"Have I got maps! Can you pinpoint the care homes for me, and I'll crack on tomorrow?"

They risked life and limb running across the six lanes of late evening traffic to the Ultramar motel. They sat on the two queen-sized beds and planned a route for the care homes.

"Jeepers, it's 2 a.m. It's time I had gone."

"I'll walk you; see you across the road."

"And get killed on the way back," she laughed, "I'm a big girl, Uncle."

"Okay, but call me when you get in the car. The number's on this card."

"Hey. Don't try to control me. In my job, I deal with all sorts of people and situations. People mess with me at their peril."

She kissed him on the cheek as she left, touching his hand and wishing him better luck this time. Colin was left in a glow with the perfume lingering in the room and filling his thoughts. Then his phone rang.

"Elvira, Hi. I rang not to say I'm okay, although I am, but to say I enjoyed tonight and I've got good feelings; I reckon we are going to crack this case together. Sleep tight. I'll call you tomorrow."

The line was dead before Colin could say, "Thank you."

Today is worse than yesterday. Not such a clever idea after all. Colin remembered the apparent triumphalism. It had taken him all day to visit four rest homes and get access to only a handful of mainly old ladies, most of whom seemed either rather too keen to help, were disinterested, or couldn't hear.

Just this last one, he thought, as he surveyed the adobe building.

'Vista Rest Home for the Weary.' Ye Gods! That says it all.

The tall, black, and gowned chief nurse recognised his accent as

British and told Colin she had visited her sister, who had married an English doctor and lived in Northampton.

"I'd love to help, and I'm sure my residents will if they can. Unfortunately, they are just having their tea."

"Why don't I show them my DVD? Not just the relevant bit but the whole thing. It will preoccupy them, and you never know; they might just see something to jog a memory."

"At least if they are eating, they won't fall asleep," said the nurse, wincing.

Colin thought she wasn't a lady to mess with and nodded affirmation.

Few seemed interested in the film, although some clapped when the nurse thanked the 'nice gentleman' from England.

Colin was retrieving his DVD and wondering if any one of those present would engage in talking about what they had just seen. Then a male voice intoned, "I worked on the 'A-Bomb.' I knew a Brit, but he was no gentleman. He was a lousy spy, and the security shot him. The bastard was feeding secrets to the Nazis or the Russians. I don't remember, probably both."

"He got what he deserved, all right." This was stated with both malice and delight, the like of which only kids and old folk can do, it occurred to Colin.

"Sorry, can you tell me again, please? I don't know your name."

The nurse butted in, "Mr Ramiraz. Georgio, this is not one of your stories, is it? He does this sometimes, usually when he's bored." To the man, she said, "I didn't know you worked at that place."

"You don't know a lot of things about me. Nobody does in this place. Anyway, it's all supposed to be secret."

"Not anymore," said Colin, who continued, "The US government released all the records after 50 years, so the whole world will know you worked there and what you did. You are one of the heroes who caused many fewer Allied troops to be killed."

That encouraged Georgio, clearly gratified at having an audience and perhaps having been freed from secrecy after all these years.

"They won't let me smoke in here; miserable sons o' bitches. Not much point in not smoking when you are eighty fucking three." He spat.

"Mr Ramirez, don't you dare do that! And mind your language."

The nurse admonished him as she cleaned up the spittle. "Mr Jameson had better be going." Colin made a temporary withdrawal.

"Is it okay if I call in to see Georgio tomorrow?"

"I don't see why not so long as he promises to behave himself. We've had enough excitement for one day upsetting the ladies like that. Come in the morning. His son usually comes in on Tuesday afternoons."

Colin took his leave.

He had just fallen asleep back at the motel when the phone rang. It was Alice.

"No, I wasn't asleep," he said, although it was after midnight.

"How's college, love?"

"College is fine, but I'm still on Santa Fe time; wide awake all night and sleepy by day."

"Have you found out anything yet?" she asked.

"Not really yet, but …"

"Do you think you ever will? Because I don't."

"Oh yes, we will." His positivity surprised both of them.

"We?"

"Yes. I've enlisted some free help. Do you remember that woman you spoke to at Bandolier? She told you about the art stuff in the State Capitol. Well, she's helping."

"Oh, and why's that? How come you have met up with her?"

Colin told her about the lady with the crab and about Elvira walking in.

"We recognised each other, and she invited me to her office to pick up the photos she had taken of us. One thing led to another, and the upshot was she likes solving mysteries, and my search for my father parallels her history, so it took her fancy."

"Well, so long as that's all she fancies."

"Some chance; she calls me Uncle."

"You behave yourself; just let me know when you are coming home. As far as I'm concerned, the sooner, the better. The grass needs cutting. It's a right mess, and there's fallen leaves everywhere."

Colin thought sarcastically that it was nice to know he was needed. *Behave myself indeed.* If only.

Immediately after he put the phone down, it rang again.

"I know I haven't woken you because you were engaged."

"El! You awaken me every time I see or hear you."

"I'm not sure if I like that."

"What me calling you El?"

"No, the whole thing; the different you. Less Uncle, more, well… Anyway, it is getting late, and I want to know how it went today."

"Well, I've got a Georgio who says he used to work on the Los Alamos project, and he says he knew of a Brit who got shot. He's a bit over the top and apparently has a reputation for telling stories, but I am meeting him again tomorrow."

"Okay, let's hope he does know something worth hearing."

Elvira said she had got an idea for another lead and that they should check out the *Santa Fe Star*, a weekly newspaper that had been going forever. The former editor had apparently retired a couple of years back named Ed Tinston, who had worked on the paper as man and boy.

"The office is behind my building, so feel to drop by if or when you call at T*he Star.*

Colin put the phone down.

"Won't I just." He fell asleep with thoughts more befitting a 16-year-old than a 56-year-old. The next morning he rang the bell at the care home.

The carer said, "Come in. You must be Georgio's visitor. Angie said to expect you. She'd lynch me if she knew I referred to her as Angie."

"I wonder; could I take Mr Ramirez out for a drive?"

"No, I couldn't let you do that. You can take him in the buggy just on the grounds of the home. He'd love that. He loves being out and won't have an audience to play up to. You'll be better on your own with him."

She took him to Georgio's room.

"Your nice English gentleman is here, Mr Ramirez. He's taking you for a stroll outside. You be nice and behave yourself and put your coat on."

Georgio grumbled and moaned as they helped him into the chair.

Everything hurt, and it was all too much trouble. Eventually, he was settled, and Colin pushed the chair and Georgio outside. Colin parked the wheelchair overlooking an expanse dotted with mesquite with forested hills in the distance. The day was dry, warm, and clear.

"You got any cigars?"

Colin grinned. *Cheeky old bastard*, he thought.

"Yes, when we're out of sight. You'll get me shot."

Georgio took a cigar, bit off the end, and spat it out before leaning forward so that Colin could light it for him.

"That's better," he said, drawing in strongly. "That's a whole heap better."

"Good, now you can earn it. When were you in Los Alamos? What did you do there? And-"

"Hold your horses, young feller. One at a time. I'm the one supposed to have memory problems." Georgio winked and spat again.

"I'm not as bad as they think I am. My memory would be a whole lot better if they made with cigars and booze. I'll tell you my story if you keep the cigars coming. Don't suppose you bought liquor. No, I didn't think so." He screwed up his lined face and absently twisted a tuft of white hair at the front of his balding head, a bit like the comedian Stan Laurel used to do.

He looked at Colin and began.

"Well, I was based in Maryland in the US Army Corps of Signals. Private First Class, more interested in screwing than in getting to Guadalcanal or anywhere nasty to fight Japs."

"I had a pack of skills unusual even for a signaller, I guess. I knew radio, and I was a sort of explosives expert." He burst out laughing.

"And I had a real knack of constructing things and making them work. I was used to working under pressure, you could say. The Army taught me radio. The rest I picked up on the street, I guess." He lay back and burst out laughing again.

"I was a cracksman. Well, a cracksman's buddy, to be true. My ole Pa was the man. He died in jail at the end of… I forget which year. That shook me, and I turned to the straight and narrow and signed up with the Signal Corps. I guess they assigned me to Los Alamos because of my mix of attr-" he stumbled.

"Attributes," said Colin.

"Yep, attri-whatever." He leaned forward expectantly.

"Come on, Mr James, whatever your name, make with another. This one has gone out with me talking too much." He held out a gnarled hand,

"Couldn't work the tools now, could I, with these? Can hardly believe how good I was." Colin handed Georgio another cigar and lit it for him.

"Let me get this right; you blew safes or were a buddy to your father, who was a cracksman. He got caught, and you didn't."

Georgio instantly said, "Oh, I did get caught. The judge was lenient on two counts. He said I had been led into the family business, and my release was conditional on me agreeing to join the Army. He said the Army would straighten me out. He was right; by God, he was right."

"Why the research centre posting?" asked Colin.

"Dunno." Georgio drew on the cigar and gazed wistfully into the distance. He started,

"What was I saying? Anyway, one fine day after I'd finished the training in Maryland, I found myself on a rail trip in street clothes with a one-way ticket to Santa Fe, a place I'd never heard of."

"I had to swear on oath I would tell nobody nuttin.' And I haven't; until now. I had nobody to tell after my old Papa died." His eyes watered, and he blew his nose.

"It was like signing up again, going to the unknown in Santa Fe, or going to prison; there was no escape. Some other guys were there, but not all of them. American and not all Army guys. There were no uniforms. We were screened, I guess you'd call it today. We were briefed. We'd be working on a top-secret project; no furlough; no going off base. The game was to beat the Nazis to the production of a new weapon, a weapon of mass destruction, would you believe? A whole village was set up on what had been a summer camp for kids. Everything we needed would be provided. I got into trouble with my big mouth."

"Does that include broads?" I asked.

"This guy came down on me like… a bomb! I dunno. Scared the crap out of me. As it turned out, there were broads on the project. Not enough to go round but enough for me." He winked.

"So that was ok."

"Some guys tried to get out, but boy, were they in trouble if they got caught or when they got caught." He paused.

"I've said enough, and I'll be missing the coffee. It's always at eleven on the dot."

"When was all this, Georgio?"

"Probably 1943 or thereabouts, I guess. What's that? Fifty-three years ago?"

"That's fascinating. Do we have to go inside? I've got something better than coffee."

"What?"

"This." Colin pulled a brown paper bag out of his inside jacket pocket.

"Have a sip of this Jack Daniels. Do you know of any other guys around here who were in Los Alamos?"

"No." Perhaps he didn't want to share its importance or, indeed, the booze and cigars. Colin handed over the bottle still concealed in the bag. Georgio looked around and took a swig. Colin took the bottle back.

"Georgio, tell me about the Brit you mentioned yesterday."

"What Brit?" The response was sullen.

Shit, I've upset the old bastard, Colin realised. He handed over the package.

"Now we are in business. I just need another of those cigars, and I'll be set up. Okay?"

"About the Brit."

"I never saw him. I didn't know the guy in your movie. I just knew a story about some guy who worked on a new invention off camp chasing Native American tail who got caught. The story went that he was shot at running away, or did he just get away?" Georgio mused.

"That's all. I just remember the story. We were told not to talk about it. It was like a corporate denial."

"Definitely a Brit?"

"Well, the equipment was British and very hush-hush. You know how good the Brits were at inventing things during the war. They went in and out of the camp only with US Military protection. Well, that's how I remember it. Nobody knew it firsthand, and few wanted to be caught talking about the incident. The security guys had a reputation for treating people badly. There were some rumours about Russian and even German involvement, but that was bullshit; security was too tight." Georgio looked around. "Enough already, Mr Whatever; I need a pee. Get rid of the evidence, or we'll both be in the hoosegow."

Colin persisted.

"Was there anything more to tell me? You said he was chasing tail as you Americans say."

Silence. Georgio was lost in his own world.

"Any more Brits, for example?"

"There was one broad from Edinberg. She was great at..., or was that after the war? I can't remember shit sometimes. Old is no fun. Sometimes I make it up as I go along. I need that pee!"

"I got visitors today; they want me to die to stop the fees, and so they get what's left of my money, especially that grabbing daughter-in-law bitch. I reckon she married my boy for my money. How about that! They will be here soon. You can come again, Mr. You're a Brit, but you're okay. I'll try to remember more for you." Georgio pushed off, self-propelled to the restroom.

Colin stopped by the office to thank the carer and said he was on his way. He reported back that the resident had behaved okay, with a little encouragement.

"What a character. I bet he takes some looking after. A real rogue, that one!"

Colin found *The Star* office by asking the coffee house waitress to direct him.

He thought there wasn't a lot of point in going to the office of a weekly newspaper, although it was an excuse to sit down after Georgio and the struggle to find a parking spot.

"Hello, shop," he said to the back of the dark-haired petite figure behind a marble counter.

"Let me guess. You are English, and you are lost." The very young pert little lady spun around on her swivel chair.

"Right and wrong."

"Well, you are English with that accent, those clothes, and haircut."

"But I am not lost. I'd like some information, and what's wrong with how I look?" He sought to look around the girl into the mirror behind her.

"Nothing is wrong. It's just the English middle-age brand of Cary Grant, Fifties time-warp."

"How very perceptive of you, my dear," was the imitated Cary Grant reply, laden with sarcasm. She smiled, clearly enjoying the repartee.

"I want to find out anything I can about Los Alamos and its history, particularly anything about British involvement. Do you have stuff on file from, say, 1943 or 1944?"

"Jeez, my mother wasn't even born then, and you must be older than middle age. You must be senior. Yes, we do have files stored somewhere. They saw the light of day after the 50-year embargo lapsed."

"Can you find out for me, please?"

"If you can give me a specific date, it will narrow down any search assuming we do have stuff that old."

"Might it be possible to sit me down with all the issues for the two years, say from April 1943?"

"I suppose I can ask. Seems like a tall order. Can I say who's asking?"

"My name is Jameson. I'm doing some research for a very old university, English, of course." He lied, and it was obvious. The pert little lady gave him the 'oh yeah' look. He stood his ground and looked at his reflection in the mirror behind her.

"How should I get my haircut then?"

"Well, I am the fashion writer for *The Star*, so you've come to the right hombre. Very short; like very, very short. Ask for a number three all over. That should do it. There's a barber shop at the end of the block. Ask for Zach. Tell him Marci sent you."

"Thanks. And, oh, can you tell me how to find Ed-" he faltered.

"Triston, Ed Triston."

"That might be easier than getting to the papers. This will take a while. Can you call back later?"

"Well, I have another call to make and a haircut to get."

"Sure." She smiled and turned away.

Colin stood and watched her pert little bottom jog as she walked into the back. She turned her head to see if he was watching and couldn't resist smiling when she saw he was.

Colin had to wait for Elvira. She wasn't in her office, so he walked past *The Star* building to the barbershop. A young man sat reading a newspaper. Busy wasn't the word today. He leapt up eagerly as the bell on the door jangled.

"Yes, sir, right here, sir." He waved Colin into his chair.

"How can I help?"

"Are you Zach?"

"Sure am, at your service."

"Marci said to ask for your number three."

"Marci said? She runs my life or tries to. And now she's running yours. She's right; a short cut is what will do wonders for you. Long and straggly is what happens with thinning hair. How did you meet her, sir?" he asked, taking up the trimmer.

"In *The Star* office, she is sumpin' as you would say."

"If you know her as I do, you would say she is sumpin' else, sir."

Elvira's response was immediate.

"The hair is great! Look at the new you. Where'd you get that?"

"Zach did it at Marci's direction."

"Who is Zach, and who is Marci?"

"Marci is the receptionist at *The Star*. She's what passes for the design expert for the paper, apparently. Zach is in the barbershop on the corner beyond."

Over coffee, Colin told Elvira the story Georgio had told him.

"And Marci is trying to find the back issues and locate former editor Ed Triston." Elvira said she would be tied up until well after six o'clock and then would have Ray to contend with, Ray Dulatti being her boss, the DA.

"Look, you do what you have to, and I promise to phone you before bedtime… Okay?" Colin left, thinking he supposed he'd be laying claims in his place so long as that's all he was laying on her. He was beginning to feel like her protective uncle and walked quickly back to the newspaper office just ahead of the rain.

"Now you're international," Marci greeted him with a grin.

"All you need now is to change the eyes. Go see the occultist and go round and gold instead of brown and square. Spectacles, I mean."

"They are not brown. They are tortoiseshell."

"Sure, but change. Just go round the corner onto Ranchero and tell Palmer I sent you." Colin feigned recoil.

"Hey, enough. I'm here for my project, not an appearance makeover. One change is a major shift for me. It might seem a small change to you, but-"

"Okay, okay, I've got something for you. My boss says you are wasting your time looking in back numbers because we were censured. There were stories, but they had to be approved before release, and zilch was allowed, but…" Marci paused for effect.

She continued, "Old Ed, the old head, will bore the pants off you with stories and goings on from those days. You wanna see him?"

"Well, yes, ASAP."

"Huh."

"As soon as possible, please."

"That's a double 'P,' as in 'A-S-A-P-P!'"

"Okay, where can I get to him?"

"You had better phone first. He lives on the fringe of town on the old Santa Fe trail with his daughter. He's a lovely old guy. He calls in sometimes when his daughter comes to the mall to shop. She leaves him here to chat with whoever is around. We all look forward to him dropping in. The old ones say it was much better when Ed was king."

She looked round in mock anxiety in case she was being overheard and grinned at Colin.

"I say too much, too often."

Chapter 10

Colin followed Marci's clear directions and got to the small house at the prearranged time of three o'clock. The house and garden looked well groomed and tidy. A grey-haired lady of about fifty showed him to a room obviously where the former editor kept his memorabilia.

The walls around the room were lined with shelves laden with folders, files, and books. There were piles on the floor as well. Ed, a Hitchcock lookalike, bald and rotund, looked over the top of his rimless spectacles. He wheezed.

"You want information on Los Alamos and all that? Lisa told me you'd said on the phone."

"Yes, please. I don't want to waste your time."

The response was, "I got plenty o' that young man, so long as I stay alive!"

"Okay, well, it won't hurt to give you a focus. Otherwise, I might be here chasing you for every detail."

"Sure, so focus me then, young man. No sense in beating about the bush.

Lisa, can we get some coffee for Mr Jameson? Colin, isn't it?"

"Yes, Ed. I'm trying to find out about my father, who was in Los Alamos in about 1943."

"That should be no big deal, seeing as the 50-year rule expired. That should be on record and accessible now."

"Well, actually; the authorities said he wasn't."

"So, how do you know he was there?" Ed interrupted.

"I've got him on film; on the official video. I've got it on DVD."

"That don't mean shit, pardon my mouth."

"I should think so!" said Lisa, shaking her head as she walked in with coffee and a plate ladened with food.

"You like cookies? Help yourself."

"They put out all kinds of crap under the guise of official information after everything had happened."

"Lisa," Ed shouted.

"Put this video thing on, will yer? I had a lifetime in information and communications and yet don't understand a thing about electronics."

The long-suffering Lisa shook her head.

"You can't be bothered to try. Just 'shout for Lisa' It's too easy."

They watched the film. Colin pointed out his father, and Ed picked him out on the second shot.

"Well, that looks as real as anything I've seen, but don't assume; don't make 'an ass of you and me' without checking it out. So, that was your father, and he was a Brit. There were some, not that I got to know of many."

Colin voiced eagerly, "He was in the Signals; in the army, not a scientist, not a civilian."

"Anything else?"

"His name was J J Jameson, same as mine. Sort of unusual; three Js in a row. It was my Grandad's joke."

"Where did he go after Los Alamos?"

"That I don't know. The mystery is that my mother received a telegram from the British War Office saying he was missing, presumed dead, but when I followed up to find out where, when and how he died, they had no record. He could never have returned to the UK. His trail begins and ends with this film."

Ed scratched his chin, ruminating. He inclined his head and said, "There was a story which was pulled by the censors. Something about a guy, maybe a Brit, I don't know. He either ran off from security, never to return, or got shot. We were threatened with closure a number of times for wanting to put exciting stuff like that out in the paper." Ed stared into space and then wheezed.

"I walked on a tightrope sometimes. You know this Brit might well have been a guy who was said to have run off with a Hopi woman, although there was loose talk about spies. Perhaps it was just people who were of unusual appearance or mannerisms. Strangers were easily identified. There were no tourists then. I reckon it was '43 or '44 when there were stories around. Lately, there has been an account published of the activities of suspected Russian spies. We reported it at the time, but security was increased. The security men were specially selected. They were mean sons of bitches."

"There were stories that never got out officially, rumours really: earthquakes, explosions; new armaments being tried out in the desert; convoys moving at night. Native Americans and Mexicans tended to pick up on these things. We knew but couldn't publish."

Ed closed his eyes; the effort of speaking had tired him. Colin looked at his watch and coughed, enough to cause Ed to refocus.

He went on, "Actually, there is a guy, still alive, who privately kept a diary of these, er, events. Military enemy number one, I suppose. He got into real hot water over UFO sightings in the Fifties and Sixties. His moniker is Romero. He's a strong character, not to be messed with. Let me see if I've got anything on that shooting or whatever. Lisa, top up this guy's coffee, will yer hon?"

Her father got to his feet and walked stiffly into a back room. Colin also got up, stretched his legs, and walked into the kitchen to Lisa.

"He's a great guy, your father. Seems on top of everything."

"Yes, he is. A little too much sometimes for my liking. Needs to slow down a bit at his age. That's what I keep telling him, but will he listen!"

"Here we are," came a muffled voice.

"I knew I had it filed away. That's why a lifetime of care about putting things away properly makes finding them easy. I reckon now the 50-year-old stuff is out, I ought to write my memoirs."

Ed scratched his face and produced a somewhat dusty cardboard box full of papers, photos, and cuttings, all with one thing in common – blue pencil line crossings out.

"This was the stuff that didn't make it in '44. The guy who did the censuring mostly was the meanest, most thorough son of a bitch you ever met. Nothing got past him – even harmless or titivating stuff. Only he could connect anything that might stop the game at Los Alamos or interfere with it. Here it is." He waved some papers in triumph.

"I told you so. Who can't remember things?" This was addressed to the pained Lisa, who smiled bleakly.

Colin read the faded piece, which had obviously been knocked out on a typewriter with a worn blue ribbon.

From our military source:

It was reported today that an English army soldier based near Los Alamos had been found by Military Police contacting and reportedly passing information to non-allies at Mel Tempi hot springs.

A spokesman said that investigations were being undertaken. The man had been under observation and had mysteriously departed the scene.

The spokesman was unable to say whether he had been passing on sensitive information and the case was being treated as desertion, a capital offence in time of war. The man's name was not disclosed. No other military staff was involved in the incident, and the senior British officer was said to be satisfied with the way it was being handled.

Ed offered Colin another piece:

"The County sheriff's office today issued a statement repeating the message that the area marked by military fences around the Manhattan project area and territory designated on the State map as, 'Military – keep out' must not be transgressed on penalty of death. He said that the statement was made to try to stop the Hopi and others from going to Mel Tempi hot springs. He reckoned that's where the Englishman might have made contact with non-allies, later to be focussed on as Russians. The only folks who went there were Hopi Indians. Al Romero never believed the story of espionage, saying that nobody would go there to receive information. It was miles from anywhere with no roads, just a track. Any vehicle trying to get there would be a sore thumb. He seemed to think the reality was probably that two guys from different backgrounds or cultures might have fallen out and that the story was a cover-up."

Colin asked, "How can I find out who the man was who deserted or got shot?"

"If I were you, I'd get in touch with Romero, the guy who kept the diary," said Ed. "He's over 80, but his son, Junior, is following in his footsteps. Between them, they are leading the New Mexico UFO sightings group. Old Romero has been jailed a couple of times for contempt and obstruction, and so on. He'll get a real kick outta spilling to a Brit, especially if he can have a go at the establishment. If you wanna see him, I'll set it up for you." Colin nodded.

"Lisa, pass me the White pages." She didn't; instead, she looked in a small notebook.

"Here's the number." She dialled and handed the handset to Ed.

After shouting and laughing, Ed said, "I've got a Brit here. Yes, a real live Brit. He wants to know more about something that happened in Los Alamos in about 1943. Yeah, that's right, 1943. It's not a joke."

Ed then told Romero the story that Colin wanted to pursue.

Eventually, he put down the phone and said that Romero would be happy to see Colin at the weekend, not that he thought he might be helpful.

"His home is six hours away, and don't expect to get away without having to listen to the story of his life's work and his theories about what the US Government is up to in New Mexico."

"Thanks, Ed, much obliged. I'll let you know if anything comes out of this."

They shook hands, and Colin turned towards the kitchen.

"And thank you, Lisa. The coffee was great, and the cookies? Mmm." He smacked his lips.

"It was nice to meet you, sir."

Colin took his leave of them and returned to his lonely motel room, and waited for a time before phoning Alice when he knew she should be home from college. He updated her on progress and suggested he might need to stay a little longer, say another week. The reply from Alice sounded as if it were code for 'Stay as long as you like.' She sounded fed up and disinterested. Colin tried amelioration; not his forte.

"Is the course going okay, love?"

"Oh, the course is fine. It's all the other things: household things; cleaning; shopping; cooking; clearing up, that get in the way."

"Just one more week, and I'll give it up if I've not sorted it. I promise, love."

"Good. I'll keep you to it!" said Alice emphatically.

The phone rang. Elvira sounded high, which niggled Colin for some reason. He needed to remind himself to keep himself in check.

"You been having a good time?" asked Colin.

"Tolerable, tolerable." She sounded as though she was playing down the evening.

"Ray's quite good company when you've had a drink or three," she laughed.

"What about you with your new hairstyle? How have you got on?"

"I've got more on that spy or non-spy story, and I've got a date with a man called Romero in Alamogordo on Saturday."

"If it's the Romero of UFO fame, I'll come with you. I'd love to meet him; well, his son, really. He looks really cute on television."

Colin was appeased,

"It sounds a long way. Ed Triston, the former 'Star' editor, says six hours. Let's go early on Saturday, and if it gets too late to get home, we can stop over somewhere. Shall I pick you up at, say, seven?"

"No, I'll drive. I'll aim for seven." Elvira was in charge.

The next day, Friday, Colin drove out to Mel Tempi to survey the scene as he had nothing else to do. He stopped where the road became a track and parked.

He thought he had better not risk the hire car. Fortunately, the day was a little misty, so for the time being, the heat wasn't a problem. It might be different for the return journey.

An hour later, he got to the action. A couple sat in water up to their necks, watching his approach.

Colin sat on a rock about 50 yards away for a few minutes and mopped his brow. Then the couple got out of the water stark naked and, to his astonishment, walked towards him. She was heavy-breasted. He tried not to look at her.

"White folks don't come here to sit outside the water, sir. It's strip and in!" she said.

Her navel was on the same level as his head and about three feet away from him. The sun, now out, was in his eyes, and he had difficulty in raising his eyes to meet hers, much to his embarrassment.

Then the man said, "That's right; come on in and join us. Janie only comes here to look at the men. She's not so keen on the womenfolk displaying their wares unless they bring a guy along."

"Josh!" she admonished.

"What will the gentleman think? We got a spare robe if you need it. Not many tourists around his time of year. Where you from?"

"England. I'm known as JJ." He stood up.

"Pleased to meet you both."

"Well, this is a new experience for me," said Colin, resisting the invitation to get wet. He sat on a rock in partial shade. Then he took off his shoes and socks and dangled his feet in the water.

"This is something to write home about."

"Chicken!" the couple chorused.

Colin stayed with them for quite a while, enjoying the occasional blatantly sexual asides from them, not so much aimed for his benefit as theirs. Clearly, thought Colin, they both get excited at the thought of Janie engaging with another guy, even if only verbal and visual. The only time Colin felt stirrings in his loins was when his mind drifted to thinking about a whole day and perhaps longer with Elvira the next day.

He asked the couple, "Do you come here often?"

"Whenever. Often only meeting up with Hopi, if anybody; for some, it's a place of homage. It's too much effort for most Santa Fe folk. Some days there are people selling stuff for tourists, usually on weekends and holidays. Midweek it's usually just us bathers."

Still immersed, Colin dried in the sun, put on his footwear, and waved goodbye to his new friends.

Chapter 11

Saturday morning, Elvira swept into the motel yard a little too fast.

"You drive, Uncle. I'm in a state. Too much of last night in my system. I need some sleep."

Colin noted she looked totally different from previously. Her hair was down; her face more heavily made up; her eyes overshaded with too much mascara. She wore a lacy white shirt and a minimal mini skirt in a tight clingy material. Previously, she had looked like a professional woman at work or play.

Not so this morning, he thought.

She got into the passenger seat carelessly, exposing a lot of thigh.

She was asleep straightaway. Colin nodded, thinking that it was a good job he was up early enough to check out the route to Alamogordo on the hire car road map. After nearly three hours of driving with Elvira breathing steadily, Colin needed to heed the call of nature. He said quietly, "Pee." No response.

The road ahead and behind was straight and clear for miles, so he pulled to the roadside and stopped. Elvira's breathing didn't change. She was still asleep. Colin got out, walked round to the back of the car, and started to relieve himself. He looked over his shoulder as he heard the car door open.

"You might have told me." she said, "I need one, too. I bet the sun feels nice on your friend."

Embarrassed, Colin croaked, "Yes, it does, and so did the water at Mel Tempi, but the company wasn't as nice. I went there yesterday. It might have been the site where someone, possibly my father, was involved in an incident although denied by all and sundry in authority."

"Possibilities like probabilities multiply; don't get too excited about possibilities," was a rationalising response.

He glanced at her. He wondered what possibility she was talking about. She gave him a look that said, 'that's for me to know and you to guess.'

She seemed different or at least in a different mood as she checked her appearance in the mirror and replenished her lips.

Yesterday's stirrings resurfaced, and he drove on smiling.

Elvira noted a sign which declared they were entering 'Truth-or-Consequences, Population 6,800, altitude 1,294.' They stopped at a roadside eating house full of tourists who were in the spa town to take the waters. They had eggs easy over for lunch and coffee, then pressed on to El Paso with Elvira behind the wheel. Colin napped for part of the way but spent most of the time watching Elvira surreptitiously. Periodically, she would twist and hitch up or pull her skirt to get comfortable. The November sun shining through the window made it hot in the car despite the noisy climate control device.

"Okay, Uncle. Tell me about you. I know nothing other than the stuff about your father, and I have met your wife, of course. Where were you born? What did you do for a living? Come on, Colin, make with your story."

"Must I? Oh, all right." Colin began, "I was born in Yorkshire, a county in the north of England. Yorkshire is known as 'God's own country' and is big enough to be a state. It has dales and moors. Dales are mainly rolling hills awash with sheep. Fields are enclosed by dry stone walls; no mortar, but so painstakingly put together by hand that they will never fall down. The moors are big open spaces, more rugged, and more demanding for hikers. As a kid, I was lonely; no siblings. I was shy; I was bullied. I was ashamed that I got free school meals on account of Mam being widowed. One teacher saw what was going on, and he introduced me to a chap who-"

"Chap?" questioned Elvira.

"A man. This one ran a judo club. It gave me confidence. I trained hard and did well. Harnessing my temper, I found released my power as well as the speed of movement on the mat. The bullying stopped, and I did better at schooling. After I left school, I was an office junior at *The Dales Building Society*. Over here, you would say 'funding real estate,' I guess. I slowly went up through the ranks, eventually being admin chief. Alice says I was a pillar of society. She doesn't see the other side of me or doesn't want to. To be a judo winner, you have to have a ruthless streak. When it's you or him, it has to be you."

"Last year, the firm reorganised, saw me as dispensable, and made me redundant, which eventually brought me to sit alongside you, Elvira. And that's it. Now it's your turn, lady."

"Okay, I was born in LA; schooled in LA; then went to Berkeley college to do law. I was head girl at school, student lead at college then recruited to the DA's office in Santa Fe, where I still am. I feel hedged in there; I need to move on. Too much red tape, although I do like the investigational side of the job. That's why I jumped at the chance to help you and Alice."

Elvira shrugged her shoulders.

"That's it, Uncle."

I knew she was a star, Colin reflected.

"A return trip to see Romero in a day is too much," said Colin. "Let's stop for a snack and work out what's best." A 'Burger and Beer Joint' appeared on the roadside, so Elvira pulled in.

They decided not to try to make the return trip on the same day, so they agreed to find a motel as soon as they got to Alamogordo and to phone Romero to arrange to see him before making any other plans. They found the Dollars Inn on the map. They pulled up, and it was clear the place could do with some TLC.

"Is it for two for one night?" asked the pleasant elderly guy behind the desk with half specs on the end of his nose with his thumbs in his waistcoat pockets. Colin didn't have to wait long as Elvira interjected.

"We want a room for one or maybe two nights with two beds, on the back away from the road; no smoking, and with a hot tub. Okay?"

"Yes, ma'am, There's a house jacuzzi by the pool, ma'am, I got a room for two for just one night, away from the road, and it's yours until 11:00 hours tomorrow. That'll be $75. Can I have your American Express card, sir?"

Colin handed over his card. He didn't ask for a AAA discount for elders as he would have done had he been alone or with Alice. Once in the room which overlooked the outdoor pool and the ground floor rooms opposite, they phoned the number Ed had given to him.

"Romero here. Who is this? Oh, the Brit. Where are you? You made it already. Great, don't eat. Come right over. You come and help us celebrate. We got a party going on. We've had a big day. My boy, Junior, won his court case against the authorities over the incident on the missile base at White Sands. The judge threw out the charges.

"Hey, and there's a lady here you will want to talk to. So come on over soon as you can."

Elvira had overheard.

"A party. I've got nothing to wear."

"I bet you've got more than me, and anyway, you look fabulous in whatever you wear. If you go dressed like that, you'll get attacked. That mini is more like a belt than a skirt." Elvira mock curtsied.

"Why, thank you, Uncle JJ," she replied in a little girl voice. She turned on her heel pulled her shirt over her head, and walked into the shower room.

Meanwhile, Colin rummaged through his bag and pulled out a less than a crisp shirt. "This will have to do," he muttered.

Elvira shouted, "You want in?"

"Yes, ma'am," Elvira walked out towelling her hair, stark naked. Colin walked past her, still clothed. He had a little more to shower than usual.

They found their way to the party venue, a heaving bar and country music belting out of a primitive amplifier system with two enormous speakers. Colin visibly winced and said, "Decibels are obviously more important than high fidelity."

It didn't seem to matter to the couples gyrating on the floor, those propping up the bar, or even those talking and trying to listen to the talking.

"You must be the Brit," said a young man in cowboy garb complete with boots, a stetson, and a leather belt generously loaded with turquoise. He turned to Elvira and, in a Southern drawl, said, "And who is this beautiful lady? I'm Junior, and we are celebrating that we have got another one over the Government, so let me find you a drink."

Colin frowned and thought that Junior, clearly smitten, couldn't take his eyes off Elvira.

"I'm JJ's niece. He brought me along for the ride and have heard-"

At that moment, the drinks arrived in the shape of champagne or at least sparkling wine. Junior had beer.

"Here, Junior. Get this divine female on the dance floor so we can all see her moves."

Colin eyed Romero: stocky; swarthy with beetle-black eyebrows and hair just tinged with grey; a strong man, a strong character, and not to be messed with. Ed had been right. Romero walked the floor with Colin to introduce him to everyone in sight. Colin noted that Elvira was alternately in conversation or animated gyration with Junior on the dance floor.

"They make a great couple, eh?" Romero's nudge nearly caused Colin to spill his drink. Then the two arrived at a table at which sat a woman of evident Native American descent, talking to two younger women. She was difficult to age; fairly heavily built with dark, seemingly anxious-looking eyes.

"And this is the lady I reckon you ought to meet, given what my old buddy Ed told me. Turquoise. Ain't that a cute name?"

"Mrs Turquoise Lamont, meet Mr... my Brit visitor. She got called Turquoise because she used to make jewellery, and nobody knew her real name. You'll want to hear her story. She's been an activist with us ever since. I'll leave you with her and her two lovely girls; okay, Mrs Lamont?"

"I guess." She turned to Colin,

"Pleased to meet yer... . Mr?"

"I get called by my initials which is fine. JJ James feels a bit well, old-fashioned."

"JJ? I had a friend." She spelled out "J A Y J A Y."

Romero interrupted.

"Come on, you two fine girls, let's find somebody for you to dance with. These two need to talk."

"What a character!" Colin inclined his head by way of approval as the two women were led away.

"He's wonderful, and so is his son, doing their level best to stop activities which are no good for this country or yours, for that matter. If he had turned his mind to anything else, he'd have been State Governor by now."

"Maybe, he should have done. Maybe, he could achieve even more with a more legit base to work from. It's typical of him to be so thorough. I'm only here because he knew you were coming. I was supposed to be back in Albuquerque today after the case result. I got my dead husband's folks to look after."

"Oh, I'm sorry."

"No need. We had fun, raised some nice kids; you've seen the two girls. The boy was USAF, like his ole man, and he became famous locally as an artist on a level with Georgia O 'Keefe."

Colin responded, "Interesting. My wife Alice is an artist. Well, she's a student right now. She was in New Mexico with me, and she went to see O'Keefe's work."

"Is that your wife? She's beautiful."

"No, that's my, er, niece, along for the ride and dying to meet Junior."

"Oh dear, not another. I hope Junior's girl don't catch 'em. She's a firebrand. Your niece seems to be getting on rather too well with him. Anyways, you didn't come all this way to fuss over those two. What do you want from me, James? What can I possibly know that you need to know all the way from England?"

Colin paused thoughtfully.

"Tell me about yourself; your life story, but first, were you in these parts around 60 years ago?"

"Yes, I was as a young woman. Don't ask how young or worse, how old! Folks don't know how old I am; it's a lady's secret."

"There's some of my story which is boring and some that's private. I can't see that anything I know will be of interest to a gentleman the likes of you."

"Okay, Mrs Lamont, I hear what you are saying, but anyway, what if we look at a short DVD I have with me? It might save us time, and it might not, but I think it's worth a shot."

They got up and went to the bar.

"I know you have a TV back there. Can this gentleman play his DVD for us to watch?" She got a knowing look from the bartender. Turquoise laughed.

"Not that sort of thing; not at my age! This gentleman says it won't take long."

Colin decided to show her the whole film so as not to influence her. He wanted the truth, good or bad.

The first time his father appeared on the screen, there was an intake of breath. He motioned her to shush. When the same man turned and faced the camera, Turquoise couldn't help herself.

"Jay Jay, my Jay Jay." She pointed at the screen and slumped in her seat.

"They killed him; they killed him," she sobbed inconsolably. Colin put his arms around her.

"I'm sorry, I am so sorry. I didn't know how else to do it." He was scarcely able to breathe, and they sat in silence for a while. She broke away from him, wiping her eyes.

"They didn't even acknowledge him. A cheque arrived every month after the baby was born. I didn't know how or where from. I was just grateful and didn't want it to stop. It did stop after I married Bill."

"I did try to get into the Los Alamos site before the money started, but they wouldn't let me in," she shrugged.

"A baby?" Colin asked.

"Oh yes, my Charles."

Colin went on, "My mother gave birth to me while my father was away in the army. I never saw or heard of him until I saw this film from the research centre. We didn't even know until last week that he had been in Los Alamos. Now I want to know all. Now you can tell me your story, can't you?"

It wasn't a question; more a statement. Colin sat back, sipping his drink. Turquoise cleared her throat, grimaced, wiped her eyes, and began afresh.

"I'm 81, but don't tell. Born into what was historically an Anasazi rock village community. We are Hopi, and the Mel Tempi hot springs were a shrine for my father and for his age group. We used to wander off the reservation; I was an adventurous teenager who loved to spend time with her ailing father. There was a period when the sheriff used to chase Hopi back, including us. My father was a lot like me or me like him. We were not going to be constrained."

"After my mother died in '42, I'd be 17 summers. When he was becoming less mobile, he used to like to have me take him to places he and his mother had been to. He especially liked Mel Tempi. The hot springs were good for his joints, stiff after years of mountain living. We hardly ever saw anybody there; too near to Los Alamos and strange goings on at Bradbury. Now it's the museum in Los Alamos. We would ride out from Zia Pueblo and sleep out for two days at a time. He loved it. That was where we met the wonderful Jay Jay. I don't know if he knew we were there or if he had seen us before. Get me a glass of water, hon. I'm drying up."

She drank half the water, put the glass down then continued.

"Where was I up to? Oh, yeah. He was wearing short pants and sneakers. He was involved in building some sort of radio station. They were so far out from Los Alamos itself, making the security easily avoided," he said.

"He was a long-distance runner; he ran with a map and… a sort of clock."

"A compass?"

"Yeah, that's right."

"I saw him talking to my father; got out of my pool, put on some clothes, and walked over to them. My father resented his presence at first, calling him an intruder on what he saw as his religious site; his private territory. I suppose it was, in a way. Anyway, Jay Jay was nice and apologised for intruding."

"My father relented when he realised this was one guy, a loner, and there would not be others following because his thing was so demanding; running long distances in hot weather. He was a shy sort of guy. There was nothing to be afraid of. He got into the pool without anybody seeing him if you know what I mean. After a while, he said he had to go. He couldn't be away too long and would have to work at night. He left saying perhaps we would meet again."

"Anyway, we left the next morning. My father wasn't feeling too good. In fact, this was the start of an illness of the head, which was to cause him to die very soon afterward. I think that trip actually speeded his dying."

"Virtually his last words were to ask me to promise to take a package to put in the pool at Mel Tempi, a sort of appeasement to the Gods for him having tolerated a non-believer at the site. To this day, I know not what was in the sealed package he gave me. It was heavy enough to have been a rock, perhaps a piece of the rock on which he had lived. I didn't want to make the trip alone and felt I was in a trap. But I had promised, and so in the end, I went. Just me and the burro with a sled and a pile of dry grasses and palo verde with water needed for a full day's march each way. I and the burro got to Mel Tempi early evening."

"I fed the burro. She had plenty of water to drink. I got in a pool and closed my eyes. My finely-tuned ears heard a rustle, and the burro stirred. I reached for my knife alongside me and sat up."

"Sitting on a rock twenty feet away was a man. It was Jay Jay. I got out and covered up. He asked where my father was and said he was sad for me when I told him he was with his ancestors. We talked. Not a lot to talk about. He got up close, and before we knew it, we were, you know, doing it, making love. It happened. It just did. It was one of those things. We pulled away. The emotions got to me, and I was upset and felt I had let down my father."

"It was getting late, and Jay Jay said he wouldn't leave me in the state I was in. We shared the remaining food I had, some bread and pieces of dried meat, and then I got in the bivouac, and Jay Jay stayed outside."

Turquoise paused, took a sip of water, "For a while. He said he would be all right. He wasn't due to work so he wouldn't be missed. After a while and being unable to sleep, I said his name quietly, and in no time, he was under my blanket with me. You can guess what happened! No need to spell it out. A young man a world away from his wife and me; an available female in an emotional state."

"I've never told anybody what happened next. In fact, I've never told anybody any of it. I have kept it out of my mind. I silently chant my mantra and focus outside my body."

They proffered their glasses for replenishment by the waiter. Then Turquoise continued, "But, back to that morning, that awful morning. Jay Jay hissed and ran up a rock face and looked towards where the road ended, and the rough track started. He jumped down. "It's the security truck! I'm in for it if they catch me. You go like hell. Leave your stuff, and get on the burro, now. Go!"

"I freed the tether; got on Jenny and Jay Jay hit her, and me and the burro we shot off. Burros are very fast but smooth to ride; anyway, I was used to bareback riding. We were soon out of sight, and as we went over a slight rise, I heard a gunshot and reckoned it was aimed at me, so I went on, head down. I reckon Jay Jay ran for it. He was a runner. I can't imagine him not running."

Colin let out a long soft whistle.

"Gosh, what a story! A story my Mam never knew, thank God. You have been terrific; any more to tell, Turquoise?"

She shrugged, "I did move on. I had to. The shame of those days in being pregnant and unmarried, and I didn't want my baby taken from me. That was my main reason for saying nothing. Like I say, what does it matter? It was a long time ago. Los Alamos was still going until 1947 and the horrific Hiroshima event."

Turquoise sat back, back in her thoughts for a while, then continued. "The Pueblo was an uncomfortable place to be as a single mother with no man to support me. So I moved to Albuquerque and started making and selling turquoise jewellery. I stayed with a kind lady who took a shine to me and my predicament, as you might say. She loved being involved in bringing up Charles. He was just like Jay Jay in looks and temperament. My friend was unable to work, and my rent was her sole income. One day, this handsome dark-haired US Air Force man, Bill, came into the shop and kept coming in! He said I had to marry him or he would be broke, buying all that silver and turquoise jewellery for sisters, cousins and friends, and neighbours."

"We married and produced the two sisters for Charles you met already. Bill brought up Charles with me, treating him as his own. Bill was a terrific guy. He didn't know my story and said he didn't want to know. I told him I didn't want to know his. He died of prostate cancer six years ago now, and I still miss him every day. The girls adored him."

"There were rumours that a Brit had been shot for selling secrets to foreign visitors," mused Colin. "That Brit was probably my father. I was conceived around the time my father went into the army. Jay Jay was Charles 'father. Gosh!"

Silence. After a while, "Are you okay, Turquoise?" She nodded. Colin voiced his thinking.

"Now, had there been such an incident as you have described, there must have been some record or some knowledge. The guy who organised for me to be here today did tell me there had been a story of a Brit being shot, which was censored out of the *Santa Fe Star* newspaper. It must have been hushed up at the highest joint US and UK levels. Some top people need to be brought to book."

Turquoise responded with, "Probably long gone by now or dead. I had plenty of time to think about it while Bill was away on tours. Mebbe best to stop a wild goose chase. I am long resigned to whatever happened. It was a long time ago."

She went on with her story. "Charles followed Bill into the USAF, making an even bigger bond between them. He spent some time in England, about 18 months around 1963 or 64, as I recall."

"Where was he based in England."

"Near a famous university."

"Oxford? Cambridge?"

"Yes, Cambridge, I think. He said he could live there. Nice place, nice people, a really nice place for art and artists. That's it. He had a girl there. Enough already. Now it's time for me to go." Turquoise started to get up from her chair, but Colin kept on.

"My wife met a US airman in the Sixties on some art course or other. Be funny if it were Charlie. Turquoise, thank you so much for opening up to me."

To Colin, Turquoise seemed close to tears, her eyes welling up. Her emotions raw, she managed to say, "Please, use what I have told you if it helps but keep it to yourself."

"Let me think about what you've told me, Turquoise. I'm flying back from Albuquerque."

"Sure, of course. Stop over if it suits you. You'd better write down this number and zip code."

"Where can I meet Charles?" asked Colin.

"You can't. Didn't I say? He was killed in a pile-up on Central near the university two years ago. Some criminal guy on the run went through lights at red when being chased by police. There was supposed to be a compensation payment, but nothing could compensate for losing my darling boy, Charles."

"Oh, Turquoise, I'm so sorry. You have been dealt a rough hand in life."

"Yes, so it would seem; three men in my life and all gone, one way or another. You had better watch out, Colin! Don't be the fourth. I still have my girls, thank goodness." She was holding back the tears, then she suddenly erupted, got up, and fled to the restroom. The girls ran up to Colin. The elder of the two, Janey, asked what had happened in a concerned voice.

"She was telling me about your brother, Charles."

"Only Mum called him Charles; we called him Charlie, and he was Chuck in the art world. She has a weep from time to time. We all do. Hope she doesn't want to leave now. We don't want to go home yet. We're having too much fun here. Your niece is a real hot."

The girls left Colin and went to the restroom to seek out their mother.

Colin found Elvira in the midst of a group of men, all of them hot and sweaty. They were noisy and drunk and in a state of heightened animation.

She seemed to be trying to make a serious point to guys who only had one thing in mind: if they had anything on their minds.

Colin asked, "Come and meet Turquoise. What happened to Junior? Did you throw him off?"

"That chicken shit. His girlfriend called, and he crawled, literally. We were doing okay until she showed."

Colin responded, "You might have had a lucky escape."

"From him?"

"No, from her. Apparently, she has a vicious streak where Junior is concerned."

Turquoise came and joined them.

Colin introduced Elvira. Turquoise gave a quizzical look and said, "I think you had better take her home. She's drunk. Look, she can't stop giggling. No doubt she's got better manners when she's sober." This made Elvira worse.

"We are stopping on for a piece, and my girls are having too much fun to go yet. When do you go back to England, Colin?"

"Tuesday, the day after tomorrow. So I will get to you tomorrow and stop over if that's okay."

"Sure thing." Colin gave her a hug and waved goodbye to the girls. Along with Elvira, he sought out Romero and shook his hand, and thanked him profusely.

"It's been a worthwhile trip, and Turquoise is a delight," said Colin.

"Seems your girl is joining forces with us or coming to work for us. You had better check when she's sober," was the host's response.

"She's what?"

"Sure. She told Junior she's up for it."

Colin was astounded.

"She's a counsellor, ain't she?"

Colin nodded dumbly. He drove the pair to the Dollars Inn in silence, or incoherence on Elvira's part. Her head was on Colin's shoulder. He half carried her in, and she flopped down on the bed.

"Come on, get yourself into bed while I'm in the bathroom, or I'll do it for you." She giggled, "Yes, please, Uncle."

She was still dressed and on top of the bed when Colin got out of the bathroom, and he started to undress her. It was clear she was only wearing the blouse and skirt.

"Come on, let's have you in!" said Colin roughly, she being in no condition to receive advances.

"And you, Uncle, there's plenty of room, and I'm drunker than a skunk. The room is spinning, and I feel thick."

He carried her to the bathroom and stood over her while she vomited.

He stood with her in the shower.

"Naughty Uncle wants to…"

"Maybe, but not with you as you are."

She wagged a finger.

"I'll remember that, I will remember that," she sighed. Colin took a lingering look as he pulled the sheet over her and got into the other bed. It was a long time before he got to sleep. He went over the agonising story Turquoise had told him. There must be a case for compensation. There needs to be an investigation or acknowledgement or admission of guilt for the disappearance of Jay Jay and the subsequent cover-up.

It occurred to Colin that Elvira, being a lawyer, could no doubt find the right approach to get people in authority to take note and act.

Chapter 12

Colin felt tired of the whole business. He woke up. It was still dark. Needing to pee, he tiptoed to the bathroom. He got back into bed and found it wasn't empty. She snuggled up to him.

"I said I wouldn't forget, didn't I?" she laughed.

Breakfast was just coffee and silence at first after what had happened between them. Colin then told Elvira the bones of what Turquoise had told him. She whistled.

"She's had a rough time and told no one until yesterday."

"That's about it."

"Hey El, what's this about you joining with Romero and his son?"

"I am changing jobs. I can't stand coercion. I wouldn't respond if somebody tried to coerce me, so I don't believe in others being coerced. My boss seeks to coerce others, including me. I don't like Ray's agenda or his abuse of power. I know how he operates, and I'll handle him okay."

"You're joining up with Junior. That will antagonise his girlfriend."

She flashed him a look of disdain.

"I'm joining the cause, not Junior."

With a tell-tale flash of anger, Colin bit his lip.

"I hadn't really caught on to the fact that you are a lawyer. I don't suppose you could stretch your portfolio with Alice and me and still pursue the truth about my father over here. I intend getting stuck into the UK powers that be, to try to prise something from under a rock or two."

"I don't see why not. The new job will not be full-time by any stretch. Romero is aware I have other interests and is prepared to tolerate some coming and going from me, so long as I am available when I am needed to front up to the sort of issues for which I am best equipped. The pay will be sort of piecework, with a retainer. I have to be available by maintaining matching diaries. It's a frontline job with freedom enough to allow self-actuation."

Elvira and Colin arranged how to stay in touch.

"Will you visit, Uncle JJ?"

"Yeah. Oh yes, when we've won. Right now, I need to pack for Albuquerque and get ready to listen to whatever else Turquoise has to say to me. Whoops! I'd better call Alice too and tell her what I've learned. Oh, I am going to miss you, Elvira. Take care and give them hell, the DA and his cohorts and anybody else you might tackle on my behalf."

Tears welled up in their eyes.

"Tomorrow is the first day of my new life," she murmured into her coffee cup.

"Thanks, Uncle." They hugged and went their separate ways.

Colin drove to Albuquerque, managing not to get lost, and readily found the neat little house which belonged to Turquoise amongst a clutch of similar ones. The turquoise-coloured finish gave the show away. It was near the road leading to the Native American hieroglyphics National Monument on the outskirts of Albuquerque. Turquoise had the lunch already en route to the table. It was the classic hot dog. She said, "I feel I'm almost back at home in the village of my birth when I see those hills through the window; that is, except for the tourists. I expect there will be more and more as time goes on."

She pointed, "That's Bill."

Turquoise also pointed to a group of photos on a shelf alongside a television and above the hi-fi. They ranged from school age to Air Force to proud fathers and a not-so-fit-looking man.

There were also photos of the three children, ranging up to mature adults.

"Bill and Charles were both good-looking chaps," voiced Colin, "But so unalike."

"I never heard 'em called chaps before," laughed Turquoise. "And you do know why they are unalike?"

"You said they were both artists," Colin questioned her.

"Oh yes; they shared a studio for a while on Canyon Road, the mecca for artists in this neck of the woods. There's a picture of both of them standing in front of the studio for their open day, part of the balloon festival highlights held every October. That will be thirty-odd years ago now."

"My wife Alice would be interested if she were here."

"Take the photo and show her; it's not my favourite. We have two or three others from other years. She will know you were thinking of her if you do take it. You can also take that photo of the sky full of balloons lit up by their flames."

"Great! Alice will love the balloon picture. I can see her doing a painting of that."

Colin picked up the photos and told Turquoise what he and Elvira were going to do.

"She is joining forces with the anti-bomb brigade as their in-house counsellor," said Colin, screwing up his face.

"Mmm. I smell trouble from a certain quarter." Turquoise winced.

"Oh, Elvira can take care of herself; professional and independent, that one."

"Okay, so what are your plans for tonight, Colin? You are welcome to stay over, but what will you do with your hire car?"

"That's okay. There is an Alamo place just off the airport with a bus shuttle service. The flight is early, so I will just get up and go if that's all right?"

"Sure, Colin, but I do get up early usually, and it won't hurt for me to hug you before you go."

The lady of the house poured coffee and smilingly said, "You know Jay Jay was a sweetheart of a guy much like you. He was respectful to my father and courteous to me. What happened, happened, and my only regret is that my emotional state gave him a reason not to leave me that night and go back to his base. Oh dear."

Colin handed Turquoise a tissue for her tears. They avoided any more talk of the elephant in the room. Colin told Turquoise about Alice and her enthusiasm for art and art history. He made no mention of her apparent friendship with a US airman called Chuck.

They went off to their respective bedrooms at 10 p.m., bearing in mind Colin's early start.

On the doorstep the following day, he got the promised hug. Turquoise buried his face in her ample chest. She handed him the photos for Alice to see. He left, hoping his map-reading skills would work.

The first leg of the flight to Atlanta was straightforward. The plane was half empty, but things changed in Atlanta. The queues were enormous with multiple flights to Europe. Security was tight, and Colin was accosted by a huge black woman of Amazonian proportions in uniform wielding a baton.

"You! Behind the line, not on it."

"I hadn't seen it," he said, flinching as the arm raised. Colin yelped and jumped backward, apologising to those behind.

What a relief to get on the train to my take-off terminal, he thought and blew out air through pursed lips. The second leg to Heathrow was long and uncomfortable, wedged in, as he was in the centre of a five-seat row.

Too many big people in America, and they all sit next to me, Colin inwardly groaned. He found Alice in her car in the short-stay park at Gatwick just before her time expired. She was uptight but mightily relieved at his arrival.

The trip home was largely silent. The busy M25 and A1 demanded all of Alice's concentration. She said, "Save it for later when I can give you my full attention."

It felt to Colin as if they needed to start over again and learn to be together. Talk over a Chinese takeaway meal that evening was desultory.

"Catching up can even wait until tomorrow, Colin. It's bedtime."

Going to bed was uncomfortable for both.

"I'm not used to having someone in my bedroom," said Alice.

Me neither. Except once, more's the pity, thought Colin.

The next morning at breakfast, he told Alice the whole story and his plans. She said that she had thought it would all be over. Dead and buried by now.

"Still, it will keep you out of my hair while I get on with my thing once the house and garden are straight. I suppose continuing our two separate ways will be a good thing for a while. Do you want to know what I've been up to?"

"Of course, darling. Successful, I hope." Colin had his fingers crossed.

"Yes, all my classmates were mightily impressed at how much I had seen and been able to do. Some were quite envious." After breakfast and having lingered over coffee, Colin unpacked and discarded travel documents. He put away his passport and the DVD on Los Alamos and saw the two photos.

Alice picked up the balloon's picture and exclaimed, "That's an image I can work with. That's brilliant! Just look at the colours. That's my palette."

Colin proffered Alice the photo of father and son outside their studio on Canyon Road. He commented that she would have seen the studio on her trip but not the blokes because they were both dead. Alice took the photo from him and drew back, alarmed. As she took a deep breath, Colin realised straightaway it was.

"Chuck, isn't it? It's the same bloody Chuck. Well, bloody hell!"

Alice was flabbergasted, "You know, don't you? How on earth do you know?" Balefully, Colin spoke.

"How could you?" and turned away.

He caught sight of himself in the sideboard mirror and felt instantly culpable from his one-night stand with Elvira. A pang of guilt hit him, and his conscience made him feel he had to alter his approach. One side of him wanted to rail at her actions all those years ago; the nicer side to play it down.

He remembered that Turquoise had said her Bill didn't want to know. He felt he had to do the same.

"I'll get over it. It must have been a long time ago." Colin bit back bile.

"I did find out, and I don't want to know anymore." He emulated Turquoise's stance of two days earlier with his head going up and down as if to try to convince himself that was what he needed to do.

"There's not been anymore, have there?"

Alice shook her head. She was in tears.

"No, I swear." Colin continued to feel guilt and anger in equal measures. He put his arms around her.

"I'll get over it. It's okay. When we've settled down, I'll tell you the complete story. I can't believe it's the same Chuck. The older guy is, was Bill. Turquoise, his wife, is Chuck's mother. Both these blokes are long gone. She has been desperately unlucky with the men in her life. Husband Bill died of cancer six years ago, and Chuck was killed in a car crash only two years ago."

"Did you know about Chuck? No? She is still trying to get compensation. These deaths were on top of never knowing what happened to my father, J J; her Jay Jay."

Alice sobbed quietly; her hanky screwed tightly in one hand. Colin took the other hand and paused, deep in thought.

"What attracted you to Chuck? Was he like me? I can see he wasn't physically from the photo, but what about his personality? No, don't answer. I don't want to know." Colin felt contrite.

"I just want to know that you love me." She nodded in tears. They hugged, but Alice, for days, was subdued, feeling as if she was walking on broken glass. She couldn't wait to get back to college.

Chapter 13

One week after Colin had arrived home, he had just about sorted through all the mail he had waiting for him and whatever needed responding to when a letter arrived postmarked New Mexico. It was from Elvira. She had resigned from her Assistant DA post and would be taking up residence in Alamogordo from January 1. Ray Dulatti, the DA, true to form, had flown off the handle and told her to clear her desk immediately. Then he changed his mind because there were things he didn't know how to handle.

When she had said she was claiming payment in lieu of notice, he had said, "You have thrown away a career and made me look stupid. I'll talk to my buddies and stop you in your tracks if you ever bring cases to court. Just clear up my work. Four weeks then out."

Elvira's letter continued:

'That just confirmed for me that I am right to go for the principles I believe in. Dulatti is a bastard. One thing I am getting on this new internet device is called email. It's like a phone call but in writing. If you can't access it in the UK, try the local administration. You may be able to buy occasional access like from the community library when they have it, as surely they will. It is unstoppable. My electronic address is 'elvira1@hotmail.com.' You will know in due course.

'I've got this buddy who aspires to be a private dick. She's bright, real pushy, and cheap. Well, cheap until we win and get compensation from the US government, UK, or both. Until then, she will settle for expenses plus $10 a day. We both get to use her and pro rata her income. You had better say okay because she is already signed up! She's good; she has winning ways; she's tiny, but we might sometimes find that we have a tiger by the tail! She has a partner, Pat, who seems to have private means, and is happy just to be with She Lai at no cost to either of us.'

Still somewhat abashed and subdued, Alice was ready enough to invest in a home computer, especially when it became apparent from the Macintosh salesman that Adobe Photoshop software, now well established, was a must for aspiring artists. The equipment was duly installed, and Colin felt equipped for whenever the email system became available. In the meantime, he used it as a typewriter and printed off letters. Surprisingly, Alice readily accepted what Elvira had said in her letter, saying there should be a limit on what the newly recruited sidekick should be paid without prior approval.

"Don't let things run away with all your redundancy money," Alice primed her husband.

Two weeks before Christmas Day, a foggy Wednesday, Colin produced his first word-processed missive.

It was a statement of what he believed might have happened to his father and about it having been covered up. He sent copies to the Secretary of State for Defence demanding a response; to the Labour MP for Leeds North; exhorting support in the House; to the editor of *The Times* newspaper for interest and possible publication, and to the BBC.

He marked it for the attention of the producer of *Bloodhounds*, the investigative series of TV programmes, asking if there was any interest.

He also sent a copy to Elvira and waited.

Christmas arrived and went. All Colin noticed was the presence of his mother-in-law sitting in front of the television, complaining that it wasn't loud enough for her to hear. Alice was more like her old self, exerting some control.

"Your Mother gets worse every year; ever more demanding. She thinks we were put on earth just to wait on her," Colin grumbled.

"It's only once a year, and it should be goodwill to men and mothers-in-law as well, you know," Alice responded.

On January 8th, a letter arrived from Elvira giving her new address and saying she had to operate near poverty and without any of the support staff she had enjoyed in the DA's office. However, she said her biggest problem was having to cope with the hostility and suspicion from the girlfriend of her new colleague, Romero Junior.

She wrote that she had to keep her eyes and hands off him. She said she had given the part-oriental She Lai Colin's address. She also said she needed money and suggested that the three of them open an American Express account jointly, that she and Colin could put cash into, and She Lai could withdraw cash from, and all three would be able to see what was happening at any time.

Elvira wrote that she knew Colin would agree, so she had set up an account. All he had to do was to email an affidavit and set up his cheque account to pay, say, $300 a month by transfer. The American Express account number would then arrive directly to him from them by email.

Elvira also said that by the time he got this message, she understood the UK would be using email, and Colin should get his computer guy back to set him up and email her. That way, she would know his email address.

Later that week, Colin drove into town and set up a standing order for $300 a month to be transferred from his current account into the American Express investigation account.

The computer man duly set up Colin, and he sent his first and succinct email, saying that Elvira's team should manage on the agreed amount. She also asked for an update on what she and She Lai were doing.

The next morning, Colin was awakened by a shout from Alice saying that he'd got an email 'thing.'

It read:

'Report for Mr Colin Jameson England UK dated January 8[th,] 1997.'

1. The search is on for two octogenarian Military Policemen who served at Los Alamos ca 1943/44.

Modus Operandi: Appeal in letter columns of New Mexico newspapers calling for former Military Policemen who served at Los Alamos to come forward. Same appeal on New Mexico Desert Radio offering a free reunion party. Visits to Facility Pentagon and *Santa Fe Star* for 'spying records.'

2. No mention at this stage of 'murder' so as not to scare off folk.

3. Meet Turquoise to ensure complete story/nothing missed.

4. $600 ain't enough. Up it to $1,000 so I can hire roller blades to get to Pentagon!

5. Reports to you as things evolve; no nil reports from me.

The advert in the 'Yorkshire Post' the following week said that on Saturday morning, the Labour MP Michael Witt was to hold a surgery for constituents.

Colin shouted to Alice, who was having her as usual lengthy soak in the bath, that he would be going to the MP's surgery on Saturday and did she want to join him. She responded that she would sooner have a walk in the woods on Sunday if the weather were good enough. He said that sounded good and suggested they included a pub lunch and that he could update her.

On Saturday morning, Colin rehearsed what he would say to the MP as he drove through the rain. There was no parking space nearby, and he realised he was going to get very wet.

When he arrived at the MP's premises, six folks were already in the room. After 30 minutes, nobody had moved, and nobody had ventured into the waiting room to invite somebody into the inner sanctum.

Colin ventured to ask nobody in particular what was going on as the frustration got to him.

The younger man beside him said that the MP had not yet arrived as far as he was aware, and neither had his secretary or whatever she was. She had apparently come in once, said nothing, and gone out again.

The others looked morosely at the two who had broken the silence. Colin snuggled down into his coat collar and resigned himself to a long wait.

He remembered that Alice had said that he should be relentless but patient. He opened a packet of Tums, flipping back to his old habit.

What a bloody waste of time that was, Colin hissed to himself as he almost stumbled down the office steps onto the High Street, now frenetically busy with the last couple of days of the post-Christmas sales.

Colin muttered, "The bastard hadn't even read my statement properly, let alone listen to me." He had had the cheek to say he had a ready grasp of my pitch but that there was nothing he could do. It was too long ago. He clearly thought there was nothing in it for him.

On the stop-start drive home, he realised it was the same old story; first, get their attention. Now, what was the story he had been told?

He recalled that a famous Mexican guru had been called in to help a village where they couldn't get their only mule to obey any order. This was the original stubborn mule that ignored shouts or even the use of a whip.

As he approached the mule, the guru picked up a rock and, to the villagers' shock, smacked the mule on the head. The mule reeled, dropped to its knees then righted itself shaking its head.

The villagers protested; why had he done that?

"I have got its attention," the guru said. "Now watch."

The beast proceeded to do his bidding, walking tamely on a lead, stopping and starting when told. Colin said to himself that he failed this time, but it wouldn't happen again. He would be relentless.

Sunday morning was cold and crisp but fine, so Alice and Colin drove to the woods, walked, and talked under leafless black branches, and twigs etched starkly against the cloudless sky.

Their breath made misty patches around their faces as they talked. Colin talked animatedly, expressing his frustration at the seemingly slow progress of the investigation. Alice spoke quietly but firmly, challenging him to be positive and reminding him how far his investigation had come already.

She told him that he knew his father had been in Los Alamos and suspected that he had been murdered. A search of Mel Tempi might produce evidence of remains.

The body couldn't have been moved without a vehicle, and he needed to do what he needed to do. She didn't mind if he went out there again to find people and badger them. She pointed out that she was back in college the next day, and she'd be happy to live in the residences and focus on the work she had to do for her MA. Like Colin, she also had to be relentless on her project.

He responded that the message had been received and understood. Colin paused and told Alice that she had really helped him get into gear.

For the first time in a long time, he hugged and then kissed her tenderly on the lips. She held his hand as they walked back to the car in contemplative silence. Something of their old closeness was back. It felt like courting again.

Once in the car after lunch at The Bishops Mitre, Colin volunteered that he wished he wasn't so far from the American team and said he was powerless and couldn't do anything.

Alice responded by saying that she thought the two girls were doing okay. She told Colin to let go.

"Delegate, let them know you trust them. They haven't failed yet."

As for the money, she told him to forget it and not to spoil the ship for a 'ha'porth of tar.' Colin felt prompted to say that Alice was right, of course, and that if they were successful, they would all become rich. He had better ensure he didn't let them down at his end.

Later they made love. They were an item again, back to yesteryear and the pre-redundancy relationship.

Monday morning was spent helping Alice get her things together, driving her to the Leeds college, and getting her installed in a hall of residence. The room was surprisingly small and spartan, more like a cell than a room.

Colin was surprised at the ease with which Alice seemed to relate to the other much younger students around. This was a side of Alice he didn't know.

Another side, he mused.

Chapter 14

The phone rang. Turquoise turned off the TV; glad, really. The soap story she was watching seemed over the top. Too many things happened to folks, exaggerating real life. Then she remembered that her own storyline was also over the top. She picked up the phone.

"Hello, I'm She Lai. I'm a private detective working for Mr Jameson alongside Elvira," the voice said and then paused.

"Oh yes," Turquoise hesitated, somewhat taken by surprise.

"Yes, and I'd like to come and see you, if that's okay, to see if we might … well, let's wait until we meet. Is Friday okay, say about eleven?"

"Yes, but… Ah, what the hell. I go nowhere on Fridays. Sure, eleven is fine."

Turquoise's face said it all as she opened the door, spot on eleven. She had never thought that a detective, even a female one, could be so small. She Lai was dressed in a shirt and pants, but it was the shoes that caught Turquoise's eye. They were the tiniest she had ever seen on an adult.

"I know. I'm small, but I jump high, and I know where to hit! And I look like my number one son's baby sister. How are you, Turquoise?"

"You are so pretty; too small and too pretty for a private eye. You want coffee? The pot is on the stove. Come in!" They sat opposite each other as the sunlight filtered through the net drapes. The room was littered with pictures and photographs.

"My husband was a painter." She Lai looked around the room, "And my son."

"Is that your son?" pointing to one photo.

"Yes. Shot not long before he was taken from me. That one over there was Charles when he was 23. He looks just like Jay Jay."

"Yes, I know. I've seen the DVD."

"You don't miss much, She Lai."

"I know you've been over it a hundred times, but please tell me about your meeting with Jay Jay all those years ago. I'll not interrupt."

Turquoise sighed, cupped her mug in both hands, closed her eyes, and gently rocked back and forth before starting to talk. She didn't notice She Lai take out a laptop computer into which she occasionally keyed entries.

It must have been an hour later when the talking stopped, and the tears started to trickle down Turquoise's face.

They sat in silence for a few minutes. When She Lai judged her to have recovered some composure, she said, "I have some questions, dear lady. Are you okay?"

"It was a long time ago, but sometimes it feels like it just happened."

"That's good. The more recent it seems, the more likely we are to get you to recall things. Now, had you seen or suspected that Jay Jay was being watched or followed?"

"No, but he was concerned about being seen. People knew he was a runner. He ran to Mel Tempi, avoiding the road."

"Did he ever say what he did at Los Alamos?"

"Not really. I know he was on a site away from the main area, and he did say when he ran, he was always on the watch for the security men."

"Did he mention names, workmates or security men or anyone?"

"I don't remember. It was so long ago."

Gently, She Lai said, "I know, and it's okay."

She rocked back and looked at her watch.

"You want to eat? Why don't I call for a takeaway?"

"No, young lady. Lunch is ready. It's a salad. Not that you need salad; a big steak more like."

"Salad is fine, and thank you, ma'am."

"Okay, Turquoise. Thanks for the salad." She Lai tucked in with gusto while Turquoise picked at bits and pieces. Wiping her mouth,

She Lai said, "Are you okay, dear lady? Shall we go on?" Turquoise nodded and closed her eyes again.

"Are you back there again?" asked She Lai softly. Turquoise was rocking back and forth. She Lai fiddled with a ring, something she did when intent or on edge. Eager to get on and capitalise on the moment, she was playing with the ring again.

"Remember Jay Jay, remember how he looked, remember how you felt when you caught sight of him. Go through what was said and what happened. Relive the good part of the day." She waited for Turquoise to stop her rocking.

"Now the men appear," whispered She Lai.

Turquoise jerked upright, rigid with one hand on her breast and the other on her crotch. *She's really there*, She Lai realised. Turquoise's hands were sweating, the adrenaline pumping.

"Describe the two guys," intoned She Lai gently.

"I didn't really see them. Jay Jay wanted me out of there. One was bigger. He was very big."

"Did he look like anybody you know?"

"I don't know." Turquoise suddenly didn't like this game and wanted to cry.

"What about the other guy? Stay with it," She Lai insisted.

"He was black – no, dark! Oh, I don't know. Mojo is in my mind."

Turquoise was crying again. She Lai put her arm around her shoulder. "I'm sorry. You've done well." She paused.

"What did you mean 'Mojo?' The stuff about the negro."

"Mojo is sort of magic. A Native American belief in some parts is that negroes are magic, some for good and others for bad medicine. Maybe I felt it rather than saw him. I couldn't say what colour he was, true to tell. What does it matter anyway? They are both probably long dead."

"One last thing, then I'll leave you alone. Did you see which way Jay Jay ran? Logic says he wouldn't follow the direction you took, which would be north. Right? It wouldn't be south towards the car at the end of the track. That leaves rocks to the east. Jay Jay being a runner, would want flat ground, not rocks. So he would have gone towards the west. Right?"

"I guess." Turquoise got up; she'd had enough.

She Lai said, "You really did do well. Thanks for indulging me and for lunch. The vinaigrette gave it a real buzz; my kind of food."

She Lai waved goodbye.

"I'll try not to bother you again, you'll be glad to know." Turquoise smiled wanly. "I bet you will if you need to. You are so pushy but in a nice kind of way."

Chapter 15

Colin was cheered when two letters hit the doormat. One was marked 'Houses of Parliament,' and the other had *The Times* logo on the envelope. As always was his way, the recipient deferred his pleasure: his excitement, his expectation, at least his curiosity, until he had had his regulation breakfast. Having broken his fast and poured his second cup of tea, he opened his first letter.

It was a disappointing acknowledgement on behalf of the Secretary of State for Defence saying that there would be a considered reply when enquiries had been completed. Colin grunted that he had got nothing more than he had expected.

He opened *The Times* letter. The Assistant Features Editor said they had enquired of the War Records Office, who said they had already answered the query directly to Mr Jameson some time ago to his apparent satisfaction. They said that Mr Jameson had mistakenly got the wrong army number. The number belonged to someone else already identified.

The bastards. The same brick wall. Colin checked the email; nothing.

He felt low. Still not getting anywhere. He lashed out at the settee with his foot in his anger and frustration. Then the phone rang.

"Mr Jameson?"

"Yes, speaking."

"Hi there. My name is Gordon Mann. Good morning to you. I'm sorry it's a bit early. I'm a researcher for the BBC programme *Bloodhounds*. You wrote to us."

"Oh yes."

"Look, I'd like to talk to you face to face about what you said in the letter. The personality of the instigator of a *Bloodhounds* case is as important to the viewers and us as the case content. The believability, if you will. The man on the street is up against the establishment."

"Your case is not the sort of thing we usually go for, but yours has tickled the boss's fancy, especially because of the possible American angle. He's very keen on that; going international. Okay, for tomorrow?"

A mop of hair, a full beard, and earrings topped a solidly built man of thirty-ish in combat trousers together with an Arran sweater. He stood on the front step grinning widely, and offered a hand.

"Hello, Mr…" He looked at the folder in his hand. "Jameson. I'm Gordie."

"I'm Colin, the chap whose Dad was killed in Los Alamos, and no bugger wants to know it."

"Oops, right, I see. I'm going to have to be on my toes with you, mate."

"Come in. Grab a pew. Coffee, tea?"

"Water's fine, just plain tap water. Have to keep the kidneys clear after last night. The team was all in Cambridge for the programme, and we celebrated having nailed the French company *Ciel Freres*."

"Did you catch it?"

"No, afraid not. Water coming up." Gordie pulled a face behind Colin's back.

"Shame. You are familiar with the programme?"

"Yes, I know of you rather than know you. I was in the US up to Christmas and have been too preoccupied for TV."

"Okay. Let's look at what we've got." They spent an hour while Colin told what he knew, what he suspected, and what was happening in the States. Gordie took copious notes. Then Colin ran the DVD.

"And that is definitely your old man? Got any proof?"

"Only the testimony of Turquoise and the photo on the shelf behind you."

"That is not proof; I regret to say, Colin. We need better than that, or we are just going to have your believability to rely on. The boss will need some convincing. Come on! You never saw, have never seen the bloke in question? You've not got a lot. Are the American police aware?"

"They threw me out, and so did the DA's office. Everybody denies everything both over there and over here. So much so that it must be a cover-up to my mind. Over there they don't deny there was a Brit but say he deserted after a spying incident. End of story."

"Look, Colin," said Gordie.

"I'll pitch your story to the boss. He decides if we run with it. Touch and go, I reckon, perhaps go, 'cos he is a maverick."

Turquoise walked wearily to the phone. She had hardly slept because of reliving the events she thought she had forgotten. She had relived the fear when racing to get away from the security guys clinging onto the neck of the speedy and surefooted mule. Eventually, the animal had slowed her pace, and Turquoise had glanced back and had seen she was out of sight of the men.

"Hello," she said into the phone.

"Hi, Turquoise. This is She Lai. How are you?"

"Well, I didn't sleep. I was thinking over and over about everything and revisiting the fear after your visit."

"I'm sorry; what can I say? You really helped me, though."

"Well, I sure hope so," said Turquoise. She Lai hesitated. There was a silence. She didn't know whether to ask. She realised the timing was all important to ensure Turquoise stayed with the investigation. She mustn't be antagonised or overloaded.

Turquoise said, "Go on, ask me. I know you want something more from me. It's okay. Say what is on your mind; I am a big girl!"

She Lai said, "Are you sure? Okay, thanks. Look, my partner's got access to an RV. We can borrow it for the weekend, and I thought we could search Mel Tempi. I don't know," She Lai faltered; then went on,

"The RV is an off-roader, so I think we don't have to walk far."

"You want me to sleep in a truck at my age. I can't even get a good night's sleep in my bed." Turquoise responded and then asked, "What are we looking for? Jay Jay's body after 50 years. It's ridiculous. You are nice, She Lai, and I would like to help, but…"

"Come on, Turquoise, say yes, please. I can't go alone, and Elvira is tied up with the nuclear lot; otherwise, I wouldn't be asking you. Please, pretty please. Just think of it as a weekend trip. It may even salve your bad memories."

"Oh, Okay. You are so persuasive, a wolf in sheep's clothing, petite with power. No, more like a sidewinder, always finding a way to get at its prey."

"I'll get to you by Friday afternoon, so we can get an early start."

She Lai put the phone down before there was a change of mind.

"She sure is smart and pushy," concluded Turquoise. "Quite an adventure at my age to go to Mel Tempi and sleep out again."

She Lai walked up to the desk of the Institute of American Indian Arts Museum in Santa Fe. She smiled into the eyes of the obviously very efficient and very proud of it woman. She frowned over the top of half glasses perched on her nose, below thin, red, almost beetroot-coloured hair.

"Good morning, sorry to bother you." Some of the frost melted.

"Hello. How may I help you?" asked the receptionist.

"Well, I have an unusual request, but I'm sure if anyone can help me, you can." The frost disappeared.

"Well, I don't know about that, but I will try," smoothing her red locks. She Lai hesitated.

"I don't really know where to start…"

"Just start talking, sweetie. Leave the rest to me." The receptionist now positively beamed.

"Well, I have this friend, an older lady. She's actually of Anasazi descent. She was raised in Zia Pueblo but had to leave; how shall I say, in disgrace. It wouldn't be so today, but this was back then, say 50 years ago. She wants to revisit Mel Tempi in particular."

The frown reappeared. She Lai went on quickly but quietly, sensing reluctance in the other party.

"She has a terminal illness." She paused for effect. The eyes, the whole body became sympathetic.

"She is fit at the moment. What do I have to do to make it happen?"

"Visiting is not a problem. You see tribes' people selling silver and stuff at the roadside, but you are intelligent enough to know that already. You want to do more than just visit, don't you?"

"You are so insightful," She Lai was almost gushing.

"You see, her lover died very young, and my friend would like to find his last resting place before… it's too late."

"Now that is difficult, even though the lady is herself Native American, you say. As for the disgrace, that will not be an issue after 50 years, for Pete's sake. Who is going to want to know?" She paused.

"When do you want to go?"

"The day after tomorrow."

"So soon. Oh, of course. I do understand the urgency; I do understand. Just wait a moment." She Lai fiddled with her ring and crossed her fingers.

The redhead disappeared into the back, returned with a folder, and said, "Why don't you have a look round the museum while I make some calls? No need to pay the $5. You deserve to get in for free."

She Lai heard her alternately mauling and then wheedling people on the phone as she herself walked all the way around the artefacts in the museum.

Eventually, She Lai heard, "But this is an errand of mercy."

"Oh, good. I am so grateful. No. Can't you send it around? No, right away, please." Half an hour later, She Lai walked out of the museum with a letter addressed to the Administrative Officer for Zia Pueblo. She didn't know at the time that the letter said that a guide would be necessary to help the unfortunate lady to get around.

As She Lai was going through the exit door, the receptionist called out, "If you get time, call the pueblo culture centre in Albuquerque just to make sure you got all you need for your trip."

She Lai drove to Albuquerque on the scenic route, pausing for a sandwich at 'the longest bar in the west' in the former mining town of Madrid.

"You don't look old enough to be in here," said the woman at the next table.

"Oh, I'm old enough, all right, just not big, is all."

She Lai's next stop was the University of New Mexico library in Albuquerque. She went up to the enquiry desk.

"Can you help me, please? I have arranged a visit to the Zia Pueblo and Mel Tempi springs, and I need to learn all about them before I go."

"Sure thing, little lady, just go to one of the banks of computers over there and get yourself interrogated. Any problems, just yell for Josh. Come to think of it, yell for Josh anyway, even if you don't need help. He goes for petite."

She Lai smiled and headed for the computer. So does my partner, she thought, smiling.

Chapter 16

Elvira knocked on the door of the Santa Fe Police Chief's office. She knew Wilma Gray, his secretary, would be at lunch. She knew, too, that if Wilma had been here, she would not have got into Justin Capper's inner sanctum.

"Come," he yelled.

She entered. He had his feet on the desk, balancing back on the two rear legs of his chair with a slice of pizza halfway to his mouth. He was a coarse guy, grudgingly respected by most of his colleagues for his effort and results. He was known as a good cop in the round with a direct and cheeky manner, untidy but homely.

"Wow! What a sight for sore eyes. Gimme a big hug. Gee, you sure smell good. You feel good too. To what do I owe this visit? How yer doing? Hey, you are persona non grata in this building. The DA will screw both of us or would if he could."

Elvira sat down, crossing her legs for the attentive audience, and then recrossed them deliberately carelessly. Justin blew through his teeth.

Elvira smiled, smoothed her skirt, and said, "Ray's got a problem, but I'm not here about him."

"What is it? Your new nuclear friends getting their teeth into some poor administration just doing their job? Why did you take up with those nuts, Elvira? You make a man despair."

"Never mind that, Justin. I'm here just to ask you, for old time's sake, to get some very old police records out for me."

He frowned. She looked at him appealingly.

"Please, Justin, please." He hesitated, then reluctantly said, "Okay, but what records?"

"Accounts of the spy incident in Los Alamos June '43."

"The what? When? Fuck! Elvira. That's impossible. You know I can't do that."

His feet came down off the desk. He paced the paper-strewn floor.

"Now, what is this all about?"

She told him about the spying incident story and the press being blocked from relaying it.

"Hell, I don't have any jurisdiction there. If it ain't the army, then it's Federal business. In any case, it's a security crime if there was a crime. And so long ago."

"It was said it was a Brit and that he ran off. What if it was murder, Justin? What if he didn't run off? What if he was shot by the Security guys?"

"Oh, so it's fantasy time now, is it? Where are the remains of the body? Fifty-odd years ago. Get real, lady."

Elvira persevered, "I've got a witness who saw two Security men. All I need to find out is the names of the guys."

"No good. Nothing to go on. And how the hell are you going to get your dear old chief, the DA, to investigate, given he thinks you sold him down the river? There is one way," he leered.

"The guy pants for you. You are all he talks about when we have a beer." Elvira inclined her head.

"Just a final thought, Justin. What happened has the makings of an international incident. It has already been raised with the UK War Office and is to be publicly investigated by a TV programme that seems to be licking its lips at the prospect. Just a thought." She left him screwing up his face and wincing.

"I can do without this, lady."

Elvira phoned She Lai. "No joy with the police chief today. I think my sex appeal must be on the wane, at least in that quarter. I think he will want to be helpful if we get something concrete to go on. Call me when you get back from your trip. Are you all set?"

"Yes, ma'am."

She Lai continued, "And seek out something, will you? Apparently, there is a report available on Russian spies from that time that may help. Okay? Good."

Elvira picked up the conversation.

"I think I'll call at the Star office and get them to put out an invite to a reunion party for people who were at the start of the Los Alamos project in '43. I might ask the *Star* to be involved and hopefully fund the event."

"It might be a this or that," said She Lai, 'this' being two or three will show or 'that' being all the snowbirds turning up! JJ will have a fit at the cost."

"Bye." Elvira closed the call.

"How can I help you?" asked Marci at *The Star* reception desk and continued, "I know your face. Ain't you famous? Seen you on TV. DA's office State Capitol. That's it." She snapped her fingers.

"Was. I moved into richer pastures but with poorer pay. You must be Marci. You remember organising a haircut for a Brit and sending him to see Ed Triston?"

"Yeah, nice guy. Professor or sumpin."

"Or sumpin. Well, we want to put out feelers for a reunion of sorts for folks who were at Los Alamos in the early days of the project. The idea is to have a free party for survivors; no, for former staff. Could *The Star* put out a notice? Perhaps they would like to take it over, fund the event, organise it, and run it. I will be with the anti-nuclear lobby, and I can ensure we will develop our relationship with them if that helps."

"I'm sure we would. Well, I sure would. The work would fall on me, and I want more exposure. The publication itself needs more exposure. I'd love to do it all. You want me to take over? The boss is out, but I'm sure he will buy it. He usually finds a way of funding things once we get an idea of numbers and can anticipate sales."

"You are great, Marci. Here's my card with my name and number. Call me and get your boss to call me as well."

Elvira's mind turned to her other role and the court appearance with Junior in the next week. She was beginning the enjoy the notion of defending clients who were tilting at windmills instead of just prosecuting no-hopers to get DA Ray's statistics high enough to win votes.

Colin read the email, feeling that moves were being made over which he had no say, but that progress was being made, particularly getting Turquoise back to Mel Tempi. Alice phoned to say she would be home for Saturday lunch and perhaps they could dine out in the evening. She was feeling low about how her course was going.

"I'm missing you, Colin," he responded.

"Me, too. I need somebody to share my thoughts with." He bustled around sorting something for lunch when the phone rang again.

"Hello, Mr Jameson. It's Gordie, the *Bloodhounds* researcher. How are you?"

"Fine, fine, thanks. Are we on?"

"We most certainly are. In fact, we have started already. We've pulled an ex-Army type to do some sniffing around. He'll need to know where to go and what to look for. He's available from Monday. Any chance you could come up to town and bring your DVD and stuff?"

"Well, yes. I suppose so."

"Good man! Claresdon Hotel, Ebury room, as soon after ten as you can make it. Cheers!"

Colin went back to preparing for lunch. Realising he needed to shop, he went to town, picking up a train ticket at the same time.

The weekend went well. Alice put things right that Colin had got wrong: cushions, ornaments in the wrong place, changing bed linen and towels. They had a great meal at the Saddlers Arms, bumping into a sailing pal of Colin's and his new lady friend, who was a potter. She was mightily impressed that Alice was doing the Masters. The party broke up pretty well-oiled.

"I'm glad the country road home is quiet," said Colin.

Alice giggled at Colin's repeated attempts to avoid the hedge when trying to reverse into their drive. Sunday was spent reading the 'Sunday Times' and tidying the garden. Alice left early evening for college. Colin thought he had better get his case ready for the show.

He parked, paid the exorbitant fee, joined the crowd on the platform, found his seat on the full train, and read *The Times* en route. The train was on time, which didn't go without notice to the surprised regular commuters.

Colin joined the lengthy queue for a cab, eventually sharing with a smiling blonde with jet black eyebrows who announced she was headed for the North End and was happy to share. He moved with alacrity and joined her. He got out first, leaving her a fiver for his share of the fare and tip. He alighted outside the none-too-impressive-looking hotel and moved quickly inside to get out of the rain.

In the somewhat squalid foyer was a board listing several meeting rooms and their intended occupants. Alongside Ebury, it read BBC.

Colin walked to the door, knocked, and entered. Gordie was there with two others, a young vivacious-looking woman dressed as if for a safari: beige shirt, beige jacket, and trousers tucked into desert boots. The blue scarf around her neck softened the look.

The man was fifty-ish in a suit and white shirt with a regimental tie. He had a stubby pipe clamped between brown stained teeth. Gordie spoke,

"Colin, do come in. Meet Sarah, one of the *Bloodhounds* baying for the blood. You will have seen her on the prog."

Colin hadn't but didn't let on. He smiled and took the proffered hand.

The Major grabbed his hand like a rifle butt and vigorously pumped his arm up and down like a pump handle.

"I am Jon Dyer, pleased to meet you, dear boy, just on board for your trip."

Gordie said, "The boss is coming in but said we are to get on with things, and he will catch up. Gail, his PA, has gone off to find out where the coffee is."

They sat down, and Colin asked how things were going to be managed.

"How do I fit in? What do you want from me?" He looked expectantly at Gordie.

"Okay. Sarah's job is that of the presenter. She will be the fountain of knowledge. She is here to make sure she gets the right feel, and being legally qualified, she makes sure we don't fall foul of the law in our sniffing or reporting as she carries the can on screen. Right, Sarah?"

"Right," said Sarah, "and I like to think I also contribute to shaping the investigation, given I am the lead on screen."

Mmm, thought Colin, as Gordie moved on quickly. *Role overlap; watch this space.* Geordie continued, "The Major here has been recruited at great expense to knock on doors and to prise them open if possible. He may or may not actually appear on the programme depending on several factors, including whether or not his expertise and authority are essential."

Gordie said his job was to make the research happen; either he did it or arranged for someone else, Jon, or even Colin. "Exactly what gets researched depends on what you start the trail off with and what we need to end up with. The boss will decide what, if anything, gets presented. We have a regular slot but can lobby for a *Bloodhounds* Special if it is in the public interest. Okay?"

Gordie looked around. Nobody spoke. The coffee arrived.

"And Gail looks after us all, Don't you, sweetheart?" Gail half smiled. "She makes sure nothing is missed out or forgotten."

"I try. It's not always easy."

"Finally, the boss." At that moment, as if stage-managed, the boss walked in, taking off and shaking his wet raincoat and theatrically dropping it over a chair.

"This my coffee? Thanks, Gail. You must be Major Jon, and you must be the reason we are here." He beamed at his own perceived cleverness.

"Where have we got to, Gordie?"

"I was just about to explain your role to Colin here just as you came in."

"My role," the great man said, "my role is, having devised 12 thirty-minute programmes every second week in which a story unfolds, starting with an untoward happening to an unfortunate member of the public. The unearthing of facts is for Gordie to sort, and the shaping and presentation of an unassailable prosecution case are for Sarah to do. That leaves the way clear for me to gain retribution for the unfortunate victim. Okay?"

"And what do I do?" questioned the newcomer.

Gordie said, "Why don't you tell us your story, Colin? Show us the film and tell us where you have got to, here and in the States." Gordie's impatience showed.

"Oh yes, especially the States," chortled the boss.

Chapter 17

She Lai rang the bell with fingers crossed, not quite sure of the reception she would get. Turquoise opened the door.

"Come in, is this…" she hesitated, "your friend?"

"My partner, Patricia. Pat meet Turquoise."

Pat, tall, dressed in black trousers and blouson jacket with cropped jet black hair and strikingly green eyes, said, "I'm the driver, cook, and bottle washer and glad to meet you, ma'am."

Drinks were served. She Lai spread the map on the floor and said, "You made it to Zia Pueblo when you fled on the mule, Turquoise?"

"Yes, Zia was my home from birth to when I left as a single mother to Charles."

She Lai said, "We should start at Mel Tempi, I think, first thing in the morning. Pat and I will sleep in the RV tonight, Turquoise."

Turquoise shrugged.

"I don't know what you expect to find after 50 years or more. Still, it is an adventure, despite mixed feelings, I suppose. It is sacred ground, you know."

"Yep, and we've got it covered. This is the letter to the Zia Administrator, which I got from the Santa Fe centre, and I also got a pass from the Albuquerque Pueblo culture centre. It says we have special reasons for visiting Zia and Mel Tempi."

"What special reasons? Tell me."

"Mmm, well, let's just say I used my skills… influencing skills," replied She Lai. Pat said, "She means told lies or wriggled her ass! Beg your pardon, ma'am."

They went to their respective sleeping quarters, planning on an early start.

The next morning after a breakfast of grits and coffee, Turquoise, with a bit of help from She Lai, clambered into the RV cab to sit alongside Pat, who was to drive. They set off on the two-hour trip to Mel Tempi, taking the US 85-285 towards Taos before turning off for the Springs.

The roads were empty, the scenery shifting from scrub to forested hills. The three were silent for much of the journey, each with their own thoughts. She Lai teased herself with 'what if' questions. What if they were refused access, and what if the pass or the letter did not carry sufficient authority? She took out the letter from her backpack and re-read it. She might need to exaggerate its authority, but just how was the question? She supposed she might have to use the attack on emotions, if necessary, like saying the older lady was close to departing this world.

Turquoise herself felt uneasy about revisiting Mel Tempi.

"Surely, things must have changed in the 50 years since Los Alamos. Mel Tempi may well have many more Zia visitors than back then. If so, they may resent the outsiders being there," she opined.

Pat was preoccupied with the task in hand and wondered if the RV might well cope with what was a rough track by all accounts. With a bit of luck, it might have resurfaced. If not, the RV was high off the ground and with good vehicle suspension, especially since it was designed for off-roading.

She Lai sensed that the older companion was uneasy.

"It'll be all right. There will not be problems. We will just take a little walk. Any ideas we get, we'll hand over to the police and let them take it on."

Pat pointed out a sign to the others.

"It says, 'Mel Tempi springs administered by the Hopi settlement association. Visitors welcome within the prescribed limits by appointment.'

"Doesn't sound welcoming, does it?" said Pat.

"Hey, look here: A coyote family crossing the road; chilling looks from the adults; sweet but dangerous. We need to keep away from them."

"Not really. They keep away from people," offered Turquoise, who continued, "I hope this truck is okay to drive on from here. I would struggle to walk in."

"The reception is over there, and here's the welcomer."

"No camping here," said a man in Native American garb.

"We ain't camping, sir. We are on a special visit with special permission," said Pat.

"I don't recognise this place," murmured Turquoise, continuing with, "there were no trees, no office, nothing."

"It's okay, hon," said She Lai as she got out of the RV and followed the guide into the office. The man sat behind a table with his back to her, his shiny black hair long and tied at the nape of his neck.

"Yes, ma'am, what is this special?"

"I have a letter from the Pueblo Culture chief asking you to allow us access to Mel Tempi on account of a lady," she whispered like a conspirator, "who has a terminal illness."

She leaned forward, "She lived in Zia Pueblo and came here as a young girl with her father."

"Well, I know nothing of this. Nobody asked me; nobody told me; nobody left a message." He fished around among papers on the table, discomforted or feigning it.

"Please find it in your heart, sir. There can be no harm; only peace of mind for a sick old lady."

"There's nobody to take you around. I am on my own. It's a sacred site, you know. I am only supposed to allow Native Indian entry."

"The lady is of the Zia Pueblo originally and left as a young woman. She can't manage alone as she can't walk very far. This is her only chance to revisit her youth. What if she were your mother? What damage can the three of us do?" said She Lai twisting a ring on her finger. It was a sign of concern.

"It's the rules. You folk have always violated our laws, our sacred sites," the guardian responded. She Lai came on stronger.

"Well, telephone somebody, the Culture chief. Gimme the phone, and I'll call him."

"No!" He got up.

"I'll guide you. Wait, I'll leave a note on the door. Just park up and don't bring any food. Coyotes don't need any encouragement."

She Lai walked quickly to the RV.

"He's insisting on coming with us. Turquoise. I had to pretend you were sick. When we are in the area, I think we need to be, pretend to be really sick, and we'll insist he phones for help. He thinks that this trip is your dying wish."

"Knock on wood, She Lai. How can someone so sweet tell such terrible lies?" Turquoise laughed. Pat said, "She'd do anything to get her way, and I should know."

She Lai continued, "Pat, take the RV back to where what used to be the track start. You'll catch up with us."

"Where's she going?" asked the guide.

"We thought you wouldn't want the RV left outside your office," said She Lai.

Turquoise said, "It's very good of you, sir, to let my friends come along. I used to come here with my father all of 50 years ago. He couldn't handle the trip from Zia alone. This site was all important to him and now for me one last time."

Don't overdo it, Turquoise, thought She Lai, crossing her fingers and twisting the ring round and round. The three set off, one on either side of the patient, arm in arm.

"It will be best to keep to the level as much as possible, sir. Are those rocks east of the springs? We should go westwards, don't you advise so, sir? Good."

They plodded on slowly.

Pat eventually caught up and relieved the guide of his patient and handed She Lai some binoculars.

"Why the bins?" asked the guardian.

"Birds, well, the roadrunner in particular," She Lai lied again.

"You were from Zia? What is your name, lady?" asked the long-suffering guide.

"Turquoise. I had a younger brother Johnny Long Hair. He left some time ago."

"Why the rocks?" the guard asked.

"Her favourite place," She Lai responded.

The guide apparently was satisfied and hung back. Pat caught up, and She Lai quietly said, "Coyotes."

Turquoise heard a shot, a single shot. A single shot could have been a hit or a miss. A miss probably would have meant more shots. A hit wouldn't have meant more shots; the odds are that there was a hit.

"A hit means blood. Sorry Turquoise, with Jay Jay dead or wounded. Either way, he would have been finished off, taken away, or securely buried to rule out coyotes. If coyotes get to human prey, it spells out danger to all humans in the area."

The guide came jogging back.

"We were just resting; she is not too good. We were talking about coyotes. Do they keep away from the Springs?"

"Only if we don't allow eating and folks follow our rules."

"I have heard of hazing in other areas. What is hazing related to a coyote?" asked She Lai.

"Hazing is the active discouragement of coyotes. Scare techniques to teach coyotes to regard people as threatening in order to stay away."

"So, if coyotes tasted human blood, they would become a danger to the population?"

"Yes. Why the sudden interest?"

"Just now, I picked up a group through the glasses. Looked like a family group near that pile of rocks to the southwest. Do you see many here?"

"No. If they travel, they travel by night. They are nocturnal animals. So we don't see them. You ready to go back now?"

"Sure. Just one thing, not that I want to, but if I wanted to shoot at them, what gun would I need?"

"What a question. You don't shoot nothing here, lady."

"Humour me, please, sir."

"Two to three hundred yards. You have to be an expert shooter with a rifle, say a Garand. That's a World War two sniper's gun or a shooter's from a private arsenal. I preferred the Springfield, myself."

Turquoise sat weeping by the pool. Her emotions were sparked by She Lai's speculation on what may have transpired.

The guide said, "You okay, honey? We need to go back. This is a tourist site. Hey, no throwing! This is a sacred place."

"I'm not throwing. I'm dropping a rock for my father. Our rocks together in the pool we loved."

"What is she on about?" asked the guide, puzzled.

Pat cut in, "Pay no heed. She's losing it. Folks her age and condition do. Hush. Come on, honey."

Pat helped Turquoise as she struggled to get up, leading her back towards the office. Stalls had been set up in the entrance and were manned.

Turquoise shook her head.

"It's not the same place. Trinkets for tourists at a holy site. My father would be appalled."

"That's progress, I don't think," proffered She Lai.

"But we have our own progress. We have a pile of rocks to be investigated, but how? That is the question. Let's get you back home, lady and me and Pat will sleep over in the RV and then head on to Elvira's. Hope she's at the rotunda office tomorrow. We need her help, I reckon."

Chapter 18

The *Bloodhound* staff listened intently and in silence to Colin's story, with Gail assiduously taking copious notes.

The boss man, Henry De Vere, eventually asked, "And you have absolutely no doubt that the man in the film was your father?"

"No doubt whatsoever. I recognised him from photos seen as a child and later. What's more, Turquoise recognised him without any prompt. She burst into tears spontaneously on seeing him in the film. There is no doubt, absolutely not," said Colin emphatically.

"Okay. Good enough for me. Anybody got questions?"

"Yes, sir," said the Major.

"I have, sir. Who in the Ministry of Defence and Army circles did you contact Colin?"

"Secretary of State for Defence and my local Labour MP. Both were a waste of time," replied Colin.

"So you have only one contact, and you have not tried the Royal Corps of Signals. They have their own museum in Dorset. And there will be Corps records at Regimental HQ," the major continued.

"En passant, did you know that the corps' motto is *certo cito*? In the vernacular, 'shit or bust..' Sorry for the language, ladies."

"I suppose that could be the *Bloodhound*'s motto! "laughed Henry,

"Although 'no stone unturned' suits me. You never know what you might find under it. We follow trails others have long given up, Major, so don't worry about going where Colin might have gone before. Being a nuisance is a way of generating emotional responses, which often are more significant than rational. Get under skins; irritate, I say."

Gordie came with, "This is definitely our coldest trail yet, boss. We are talking 50-odd years. Surely we have to reaffirm our decision either to continue or withdraw before doing anything else."

"I have reaffirmed, and so has Sarah."

"Right. Just testing, boss."

"I'll worry about the Beeb, Gordie, old son. I sniff an incredible injustice here. Even if we fail, we will have generated tremendous audience interest and figures. It's got all the ingredients -- wartime interest, human interest, tilting at the establishment. What do you think, Sarah? Still with me?"

Gordie persisted.

"Evidence, if any, is 50 years old; Will any witnesses still be alive, I ask. Without either, there is no trail and no progress."

"Yes, Henry. Gordie is right to check out our commitment and the reasons for that commitment. We want Colin to go away knowing that we have challenged our thinking and not been found wanting. I'm still for it, wholly," said Sarah. Gordie sniffed.

"So be it."

"Colin, you will be available for takes?" Henry's question closed the matter. He moved on.

"Let's go after a retraction from the Government and compensation for Colin for the lies and the denial of his father's existence. How's this: 'The pursuit of the man who never was from the city that never was."

"Appearing on a TV screen doesn't sound like me.."

"You have no worries, Colin. You are a reluctant frontman, a reluctant victim; just being you will win you some followers. Just be you, and folks will respond; trust me. Right now, I need an overview of what is happening on both sides of the pond. Use the flip chart, Colin. I'll give you ten minutes."

Colin proceeded to list on the blank chart:

Elvira: former Asst DA, part-time tackling Santa Fe police for names of 1943 Security men.

She Lai and partner Pat: private eyes investigating Mel Tempi with Turquoise, the sole witness.

115

Santa Fe Star newspaper: organising a party for ex-Manhattans to shed light on 1943 events.

Major Jon: Army and Ministry of Defence seeking to prise out the military history of my father.

Gordie: to investigate named Manhattan spy reports.

Colin: to feed US data to *Bloodhound* and push MP to take up the case in the House.

Sara: to seek and pull together feedback from all parties.

Henry: front for Beeb. Lead. Procurer of funds.

Gail: focal point; conduit. Daily call-in.

"Copy that for me, Gail. We'll run with it. Meet in one week here." With that, the big man swept out; delegation done.

Colin reflected on the meeting as he got on the train on his way home. It was still drizzling. His mind wandered. He had once joined a lone passenger in a compartment. The man was dressed in a scruffy mac and sat behind a newspaper. The man's fingernails were dirty. He wore a trilby, and Colin recognised him.

"I know you. You are my wife's favourite comedian."

"Oh yeah?" The paper stayed up in front of his face.

After a couple of minutes, it went down.

"Okay, if you want to talk, so long as we talk about you and not me."

"Right."

Then the comedian proceeded to talk about himself. He appeared in Harrogate and Leeds every evening. He said he hated being away from home and spent days in a hired car touring Yorkshire or sitting in daytime cinemas. On this particular day, he even took a trip to see a friend in London because he was due on stage until late evening.

Colin realised that he was a sad, insecure man who had to be funny for a living. His own concerns about his missing father and his disappointment over Alice's indiscretion were nothing compared to his. His mind went back to the meeting with the *Bloodhounds* and having mixed feelings, including some of Gordie's. Both he and Gordie tended to ask 'what if' questions. However, Colin had bowed to the enthusiasm of Henry and his belief in the power of television to get an audience response.

Major Jon had put in several calls from the hotel and set off to catch a contact at the Ministry of Defence before the latter set off for a Caribbean holiday.

He was positive and clearly not a man to hang about.

Sarah, for her part, was to prepare a trailer to go out on the back of a *Bloodhounds* programme, calling for contact from anybody who had been in the Royal Signals at Catterick in 1941/42. She would aim this at children, grandchildren, and the men themselves.

Colin thought this to be a long shot and that the Major would probably do better in targeting the records people. His thoughts ran to wondering how the US girls were getting on. The notion of compensation loomed bigger if an unlawful killing in the States was eventually proven.

He decided to email the American team when he got home to find out and also tell them about *Bloodhounds*.

He looked down over Crimple Valley as the train crossed the viaduct outside Harrogate and wondered how he would cope in front of the cameras.

"Not my scene; definitely not my scene." The man sat nearest glanced at him.

"Beg your pardon, old man. I didn't catch what you said."

"Not my scene. It's too much." Colin smiled to himself.

"Talking to myself; I must be getting old."

There was a message on the phone from Alice to ring her back.

She needed some TLC as things were pressing on her at college. She had aborted a piece of work in the light of tutor criticism. There was also an email from She Lai. She had made an approach to get the police to follow up at Mel Tempi, but it would need all the persuasive powers she and Elvira could muster as well as any pressure which could be brought to bear from both sides of the Atlantic. Guardedly optimistic, but some smidgeon of progress at least.

Colin surmised that he could get over there, but there was the *Bloodhounds* affair and that it was probably too soon anyway.

He couldn't offer much anyway. He had no value to add at this juncture.

Colin started to dial Alice's number, then put down the phone, uncertain again. It was his stock-in-trade. Not much point in phoning before evening. So he decided he would drive to college the next day. He had nothing else to do; he felt restless. All he could do was wait. Alice jumped at the idea of him visiting her.

They lunched at the college. Alice unloaded her concerns which seemed to have melted somewhat after a belated session with her tutor.

"At least my worries got you to come here," she laughed and continued, "That's a good outcome. Tell me about your world. I know you are dying to."

Colin said, "All right, here goes. Elvira, She Lai, and her partner Pat are working with Turquoise on Mel Tempi. They might have a lead for the police to take up. They are also setting up a free event for any former Manhattan staff to attend to see if anybody can recall anything relevant to our search."

"The TV programme is taking up the case of the man who never was. They reckon they might be putting me on the show. What a joke; definitely not my scene. They have recruited a retired Major to chase up military records, and I am to put pressure on our MP to raise the case in Parliament. Come to think of it; now I've voiced it to you, love; it does feel like progress."

"I should say so. I am impressed, but you on screen? No way."

Alice kicked off again.

"Back to my hardworking mundane world. I have to produce a dissertation on the place of graffiti in contemporary art. The deadline is tight because my tutor was critical and then went absent."

Colin laughed, "Well, they put a bloke in prison for putting graffiti on motorway bridges in Yorkshire, so you had better watch you don't get charged for inciting others to do it!" The longer the day went on, Colin became more concerned about taking his leave of Alice without antagonising her.

* * *

As it was, he got back home just in time for the *Bloodhounds* programme at 8.30 p.m. At the start of the programme, Sarah, looking elegant and assured with her hair up and wearing a tight black evening dress, announced there would be a plea to viewers for information to help research for a future programme. That plea would be aimed specifically at men and women or their descendants who may have served with the Royal Corps of Signals and were in Catterick camp in 1941/42.

The slickness of both Henry and Sarah on-screen contrasted with the flat pitch from Gordie in his analysis of research done on the case running currently. He seemed happier with numbers than with words.

Back in Alamogordo, Elvira had a sudden pang of conscience. She hadn't been in touch with Marci at *The Star* for a while. She had meant to call her.

"Hi Marci, sorry I've not gotten back to you sooner. How are you doing with the reunion?"

"Hello, ma'am. I am doing just great." The enthusiasm shone through.

"We're nearly all set."

"Wow, that's wonderful."

Marci went on, "It's not all good news on the money front, though. I've been able to swing the transport, buffet, and entertainment costs onto *The Star* on the grounds that we have sole access to the participants for what might turn out to be a big story. A few folks may need to stay overnight, so I'm aiming to get a special rate at the Adelphi. We can't ask guests to pay."

"Send the bill to me," said Elvira, who continued, "I'll talk to Colin. You mentioned entertainment and how many guests?"

"I've got 47; no 46. I heard this morning that one guy had died. His wife had said he was terminally ill but had been desperate to come. She is still intent on coming, though. About entertainment, let me run through the day, February 5th: Everybody gets a bus or car ride to the Adelphi Hotel, where they get coffee and doughnuts. The coach to Los Alamos will leave at 10.30 am."

"There's a museum tour and video, followed by buffet lunch during which there will be a talk from you, me, and Colin. There should be time for us to have one-to-one sessions with any folks with links if there are any. And that's about the whole caboodle."

"Brilliant! You are *the* Star employee and a star in your own right."

"Thanks so much, Marci."

Elvira emailed Colin and She Lai, updating them and asking if they would be coming to the event. Colin telephoned Alice.

"Remember I told you the *Los Alamos Star* girl, Marci, is organising a reunion of Manhattan former staff on 5th February. Do you fancy going, love?" asked Colin with his fingers crossed, having popped a Rennie in his dry mouth.

"Well, yes, but for how long? It's half term. I can manage a week, I reckon."

Colin sighed with relief. He was on tenterhooks because he was desperate to go.

"Can we do it? Can we get flights?" Alice asked.

"Well, say yes, and I'll find out."

"Well, okay then. Yes."

Later, Colin phoned Alice again.

"We fly Sunday 2nd February, returning on the 9th. Okay, love? It's Heathrow to New York, then to Albuquerque. We hire a car and drive on to Santa Fe in time for bed at the Adelphi Hotel on 3rd February, giving us 24 hours to catch up with ourselves. Then it's on to the reunion."

"Sounds hectic. Hope it will be all right."

"Of course, it's going to be all right!" said the positive side of Colin. It was the side that Alice had not been introduced to up to now. He took a Rennie just in case.

He emailed Elvira the news saying that they needed to be careful not to give anything away about the 'you know what' misdemeanour.

* * *

Pat found She Lai in tears when she got home from her part-time volunteering role in a local hospital.

"What is it?" asked the concerned Pat.

"Read the letter."

It was a 'come at once' letter from She Lai's mother in San Francisco.

"Another one of your Mother's panics. You always go running, and there's nothing ever really wrong, "Pat disdainfully said.

"She's my Mum. I have to go. I can't risk it."

"Well, go right away. The sooner you go, the sooner you get back."

Pat picked up the phone and called the airport in Albuquerque. After a short wait and after two conversations with different airlines, Pat announced, "There's a flight in three hours, so you have got only an hour to spare. I'll drive you. Call me when you are coming back, and I'll also pick you up."

She Lai wiped her face.

"What would I do without you, angel?"

"Just don't think about it. Hey, missie, just get back as soon as you can."

En route to Sunport for the flight, She Lai said, "If you get bored, Pat, there is an angle you might like to pursue which will save me time."

"Oh yeah! Like what?"

"Like it seems conceivable to me that the pile of rocks to the South West of Mel Tempi…"

"Oh, we are back there, are we?"

"No, you don't have to go there, Pat. Just go to any photographers on Canyon Road and look up old photos in the cultural museum."

"Looking specifically for what?"

"Photos which include the rocks we are interested in, dating before 1943. If we find photos, we can compare shapes. It seems conceivable to me, Pat, that if rocks were removed to accommodate a body, maybe they have not been replaced exactly as they were."

Pat sighed resignedly.

"I suppose. You and your tidy mind. No stone unturned. What do I tell them?" asked the none-too-happy Pat, who would sooner be making the trip with her partner.

"Just say you are interested in the geography and geology of the area. There might well be pictures of Native American religious ceremonies with a south-westerly background. Just give it your best shot, sweetie."

Pat grimaced.

"Have a good flight taskmistress. Hope your Mum is okay."

Pat decided to go straightaway to see if Turquoise knew of any religious events at Mel Tempi from her past. Pat cell-phoned her. Turquoise was not best pleased but okayed a short visit. She said that Anasazi religious celebrations would be held in kiva caves. Hopi events would be in Arizona, not New Mexico. The only possibility might be Mexican incomers, for example, celebrating Cinco de Mayo.

"Mexican Independence Day, May 5th?" Pat asked.

Turquoise said, "I have never heard of such celebrations in my time. My father would have known and been very angry had there been. Perhaps the Mexicans just did it spontaneously."

"I hope not. I need, no; we need photos."

"I don't understand," frowned Turquoise.

"Don't worry, hon. If we are lucky and find photos, we may be able to bring you good news instead of questions for a change. You will be at the reunion party?"

"You betcha," said the older lady.

Pat drove the sixty miles to Canyon Road and then slowly passed the artist studios and shops closed for siesta. She saw just two photo shops. Their windows seemed preoccupied with the balloon parades and geared more to tourism than art or even geography. One shop opened up as she went by. She stopped.

"Say, sir, you wouldn't have old photos of Mexican interest from the old days, would you?"

"How old, Miss?" he asked hesitantly, not knowing if that was the right title.

"Pre-war, pre-1940s."

"That old? No, and definitely not Mexican. No call for Mexican. The guy across may have something. His, er, woman is from Mexico. She may know if there are any around."

"Thanks, sir. Now you have a nice day." She left him scratching his head, bemused.

The Mexican lady thought the museum was the best bet. They had old photos probably of cultural aspects of most incoming residents.

Pat drove to the Santa Fe cultural museum and encountered She Lai's old adversary, the coloured hair receptionist looking over the top of her spectacles.

"May I be of assistance, Miss. It is Miss, isn't it?"

Pat laughed. She was used to such comments.

"You betcha, ma'am."

"I particularly want to see old photos of Mel Tempi and any Mexican-related activities there."

"That's a tall order. Mel Tempi is an Anasazi holy site." They would not be welcomed.

"Perhaps say, some Mexicans snook into the site to secretly celebrate Cinco de Mayo, for example," responded Pat.

"To my certain knowledge, I doubt it, but you are welcome to look for the price of the entrance fee. That's $5, er, Miss. Is there a cupboard on the top floor, or is it in the basement? The security guy will show you where. It's full of old handbills and photos. You are welcome to wade through them if you wish. Just leave as you find is all I ask."

Pat left at closing time, unfinished but deciding to return the next day. She resumed the massive task and got nowhere. She left, singing out a 'thank you' and saying that she might be back. She went round to *The Star* office.

"You must be Marci. I'm with She Lai; who is with…?"

"Elvira. You are Pat, and you are coming on 5th February?"

"That's right. To cut to the chase, sweetie, I need to know of anyone who knows about pre-war World War Two Mexican celebrations held illegally at Mel Tempi."

"Have you tried the Canyon Road photo studios? After the release of documents 50 years after the events at Los Alamos, we gave away a load of photos with a copy from the uproar caused by Mexicans celebrating 80 years of independence from the French. They were handed to the police, and the perpetrators were given sentences for causing the uproar and trespassing. I read it. It just caught my eye."

"I've gone," said Pat turning on her heel.

"Thanks. They lied to me. They won't next time."

The Mexican woman was worried when Pat returned.

"I didn't want trouble."

"Okay," said Pat, "do I have to go to the police or have you got photos of the debacle in 1942 which put Mexicans in jail?"

"I have copies. You are welcome to them; they're more trouble than they are worth."

She produced an A1 carrier, and Pat left with it. There were two large grainy black and white pictures of perpetrators dancing, with one shot including the rock pile in the background. On the back, handwritten, was 'Police evidence May 5, 1942.'

I wonder, mused Pat, mighty pleased with herself.

She called Elvira, but she was not available. Pat needed a current photo of the group of rocks and probably a photographic expert to compare the two shots independently. Elvira, no doubt, could fix that. Pat kicked her heels, willing She Lai to phone.

She Lai did phone the following morning.

"Good news. Mum is much better, aren't you, sweetie? Yes, just a little TLC and a quart of gin raised her spirits. So, I will be on the first south-western flight. Walk-on time 10:00 hours via Phoenix, so e.t.a. 14:00 hours, give or take. Oops. Mum's shouting; I'd better go. Meet me?"

"You betcha, hon."

Alice and Colin were pretty fed up by the time they got to the Adelphi. Almost everything that could go wrong on the trip did. The take-off from Heathrow was delayed not once but twice. First, some passengers complained of the smell of petrol. All passengers had to leave the plane with their take-on luggage.

Then a woman forgot she had brought an extra bag, so it was not claimed and was therefore regarded as suspicious. Fortunately, the long flight gave the captain time to catch up, and as he explained over the intercom, he had to balance speed with fuel economy.

Then after landing at Newark the next morning, they had to refuel, which meant a two-hour delay for passengers going on to Albuquerque.

They flopped onto the bed without food or unpacking and fell fast asleep, only to be wide awake at 3 a.m.

Over breakfast, Alice decided she would spend Monday with Colin sooner and then stay in Santa Fe and visit the art centres again. She had done Los Alamos and couldn't see herself being an aid to the team. Colin raised a half-hearted objection but then agreed, subject to him making contact with Elvira and She Lai. He did this while she put out feelers in the hotel to find out what might be happening in the art world. They did the art tour. Eventually, they landed back at the hotel.

"That was a long day, Alice, love."

"It went all too quickly for me." They had avoided Canyon Road.

"You do have tomorrow." Colin popped in a Tums.

The next morning found Colin, Alice, Elvira, She Lai, Pat, and an excited Marci around a table, talking. Colin deliberately sat well away from Elvira.

Alice said, "I'm off to do the galleries. Hope the day goes well for you all." She kissed Colin and said, "Nice to see you again, Elvira. You've got plenty to talk about, and I've got plenty to do. See you tonight, love." And off she went.

"Happy as Larry," said her spouse, relieved. Elvira and Colin shared a look.

An excited Pat was full of herself.

"I've got something new to tell you all."

"Oops, Pat. First things first. Can we just ensure Marci has everything she needs for today's event?" Elvira said, turning to Marci.

"Perhaps you want to meet and greet your guests?"

"Well, I'd love to be in both places, but I need to make sure guests and staff have all they need, so I'll leave you to it." Marci left.

"Now?" asked Pat. Elvira said, "Well, I think we should start at the beginning. That for me is your Mel Tempi trip with Turquoise."

"I suppose. I'll have more coffee while I wait," Pat shrugged.

"That's me, then, Elvira."

She Lai began by saying, "Best if I voice my conclusions first. We may not have time for me to do the whole spiel now." She began, "I believe Jay Jay was shot. If the bullet didn't kill him, he was dispatched and buried under rocks 200 yards to the southwest of Tempi. Pat may have news on that." Pat nodded vigorously.

"The body may or may not have decomposed depending on the nature of the ground. I have found it reported that there are examples of both in New Mexico burial sites. We know two security men were involved. We need to persuade the authorities to open up those rocks. That we reckon is for you, Elvira, to chase up. For comparison, I sent Pat to seek out photos of the southwest side of Tempi taken before and after 1943. I wanted to see if the rock assembly had changed or had been changed. Over to you, Pat."

"Yes, Missie. I have this." She pulled out the grainy black and white photo, putting it on the table.

"You can see the rocks in the background." Then she showed the back of the photo.

"Note the date. The 80th anniversary of the French defeat by the Mexicans was the biggest event in the history of Mexico. No wonder the Mexican exiles in Santa Fe turned out to celebrate, albeit trespassing in the process. A good job for us too. It means we have a photo we may be able to make use of. We need a photo post-1942 for comparison with this one, and we need this one enhanced if possible. I reckon that is another task for Elvira to sort, too."

"Well done, Pat," said Elvira.

"Over to me then. Colin, what about your end?" He cleared his throat.

"Looks like I am going to be on UK TV in a programme called

Bloodhounds, which investigates lost causes. They have agreed to take up the case. An ex-Army type is chasing up Defence Ministry sources as well as Army records."

"We hope the programme will get Brits who were training with the Royal Signals training around 1942 to come forward just as we hope we get people from here today."

Elvira said, "Wow, sounds good, Colin. We do seem to be going apace. Now, if you can manage without me, I'll get on with my bits straightaway."

Elvira left just as Marci returned.

"It's looking good. Well done, girl. I must leave but will be here when you all get back tonight."

The remaining four then became diligent hosts for the arriving delegates. All of them were elderly. Most needed help to get out of vehicles and into the Adelphi.

"It's like trying to herd cats," said Marci. "If only I'd known what I was letting myself in for, and we haven't got to Los Alamos yet!" she joked.

"Mind you; I would still want to have done it!"

On the bus to the research centre, Pat attempted to get the old folks to say individually who they were, what they did at Los Alamos, and when they were there. She soon aborted the attempt. Deafness and preoccupation with one-to-one conversations got in the way.

Marci gave Pat a list of names for her to pick up at the venue and said, "At least we got 40 of them and four of us on board. It seems like a major achievement to me."

Colin yawned. He was still feeling the effects of jet lag.

"Remember me, Brit?" It was Georgio Ramirez.

"I've only come for the drink and cigars."

"How are you, Georgio?" Colin groaned inwardly as the old guy proceeded to tell him loudly and at some length. She Lai interceded and pulled Colin away.

The event seemed to go well except for mislaying guests who had got lost on interminable trips to restrooms. A janitor came out of the men's room laughing at an oldie who had been trying to dry his hands under the condom machine and couldn't get it to work.

Surprisingly there were more women than men. Some couples and some ladies on their own claimed to have been married or otherwise related to former Manhattan project workers. Several were like Georgio, along for the ride and the party.

Only Georgio recognised Colin's father from the video.

She Lai had the playback frozen with his face on the screen and told the guests that this Brit had gone missing from Los Alamos in 1943. Georgio was the only one who knew of the story.

The guests ate their meal and remained at the tables to be entertained.

The cowboy singer claiming to be the fastest banjo player in the West went down particularly well as most of his material was from the 50s. The young comedian was less successful as his jokes were largely contemporary and not on the same wavelength as his audience. Hearing was an issue, too. At the end, they trooped off to the coach, and most fell asleep, including Colin. Georgio Ramirez got off, expressing his disappointment at not being offered whiskey or cigars.

"I preferred you coming to see me, Brit. Will you be coming again? I just might remember something more."

"I just might. It depends," Colin sighed. *Then again, I might not,* he thought.

Back at the hotel, Alice languished in a bath into which she had liberally poured all the bath oils provided.

"This is heaven," she sighed, reaching for the glass of Californian white wine.

When the four had seen all the guests off the premises except for the two staying overnight in their own transport, they joined Alice in the lounge. She sat refreshed in her little black dress. She was talking to a couple whom she had seen earlier browsing the extensive art shops and studios on Canyon Road. They were describing a painting they had paid for and which was to be shipped to their home. It sounded stereotypical of the Indian images done for tourists: a desert scene with turquoise and gold elements incorporated.

"Not my scene, but beautiful nonetheless," Alice closed the conversation with a smile and turned to the somewhat subdued four.

"How's your day gone, darlings? Mine's been brilliant."

"Everything went like clockwork, thanks to this fantastic young lady." Colin nodded towards Marci.

"On the other hand, to date, not a lot to show for the event, in terms of what we'd hoped for. But you never know with old folk. Something may prompt a late recall from someone, probably at 3 a.m. That's what happened with Turquoise, thanks to She Lai working with her. So you never know, do you?"

It felt like a gentle letdown, for Marci's sake.

Elvira, dressed to the nines, walked in as Colin spoke.

"A so-so day then. I have had the same. We got nowhere on the idea of a rock dig, although there's no point until we know there have been the changes suspected by She Lai. That will be the time to go for it big time. Is that not so?" She paused.

"Hello Alice, how's your day been? Have you produced lots of masterpieces from your last visit to New Mexico? I sensed you were inspired at the Monument." Colin was on tenterhooks.

Elvira continued, "Okay. I have found, or rather Junior Romero has located, a colleague of the photographer who does the publicity stuff for the Nuclear group. This guy specialises in the restoration and enhancement of historical documents. By all accounts, he's a wizard in his field. We: Junior and I hope to see him tonight. The publicity photo guy does have some pictures he reckons we can use for comparison. He just has to find them. Now I must go. I have a date. Keep me informed, guys, and wish me luck."

She sashayed away towards Junior, who was in a tuxedo, standing in the foyer.

"Who wants a drink?" Colin beckoned the waitress.

"I do!" was the chorus.

Chapter 19

As they breakfasted at the Adelphi the next morning, a woman aged about fifty walked into the restaurant and joined Colin and Alice. She handed over an envelope marked, 'to whom it may concern.'

"You met my father yesterday, Len Martin. What you don't know is that he is in terminal decline; a matter of weeks, his medico says. He felt unable to voice anything yesterday, but he is most keen for you to get this. Colin said " there was one chap who did look rather poorly and seemed to eat nearly nothing."

"That sounds like Dad. Can I tell him you have read it?"

Colin tore open the envelope and responded after seconds.

"Oh yes, and thank you. So sorry for your situation. We wish you and your father the best in what you have left together."

The letter in spidery handwriting started:

'To whom it may concern.

I am grateful that I have come to find God at this late stage in my life. He gives me comfort in this, my hour of greatest need.'

Colin murmured, "Come and look, Alice."

"After leaving college, I worked in a small shop. To my eternal shame, I started taking small amounts of money from the till, which had no register, making it easy to get away with. The owner didn't notice, so I took bigger and bigger amounts."

"After about four months, he said he had to give up the business as he couldn't afford to buy new stock. He actually gave me money because he could no longer employ me and I am appalled to say I took it. This episode persuaded me to join the US Army as a military policeman as soon as I was 18. That was in 1940. How cynical was that?"

"The second failure still haunts me. This time I stood by as someone else committed a heinous crime on my watch, and I did nothing. I was cowardly. Not only did I do nothing, but I did not tell the truth about what happened. I was assigned to Los Alamos in 1943 as a security guard for the developed Signals Corps radar site."

"Part of my induction was to accompany established pairs of guards on patrols in order to learn the ropes. I went out with Big Jo Paloma, nicknamed Chicago Jo, and a local known as Mojo. He was a designated sharpshooter and carried a Springfield rifle on patrol. They had me drive them to Mel Tempi and said I was to stay with the car while they walked up the last of the track and into the Springs and to sound the horn if anyone showed. They whispered so that I didn't hear. But I did hear something about an old native Indian guy with a daughter."

"This is my confession: I felt they were up to no good. Paloma was not a nice guy. In hindsight, I think they knew of someone from the Radar set-up leaving the site, perhaps to meet someone at Mel Tempi. It was hot in the car, so I got out and sat on the ground, shady side. I heard Paloma shout. "There he is. Get him!" Gunshot sounded."

"I got him!"

"I got up and ran around. They were running towards a pile of rocks with no sign of anyone. Then Mojo came running back."

"Put this in the trunk and gimme the trench tool. Jo finished him."
"Who?"

"Who? Some Brit. We need to hide the body, real secure, right."

"I followed Mojo at the double. They waved me to stop where I was, then shouted to give them a hand to lift rocks."

"If you so much as say something in your sleep, I will slice off your head and kick it down the road. You got me?" Paloma growled. "You believe me? That's if Mojo hasn't blown it off already."

"Paloma jabbed a bowie knife into the sand several times to clean it. He then told me to get the shovel, scatter the sand from the base of these rocks, and then throw on some fresh sand from behind. Paloma then said, "Just think on, Lennie boy. You are now an accomplice to murder. It's still a hanging offence in this State, so keep your mouth zipped."

"That I have done until now, and I am so, so sorry and so ashamed. May God forgive me."

Colin read on.

"I got transferred to the security admin centre on Sergeant Paloma's say-so as unfit for patrol duty. I was relieved at that. This is my dying admission of complicity in killing a man at Mel Tempi in 1943. This, I swear by Almighty God, is true.

Signed, Len Martin date 02.05.1997

Signature witness; Nurse (name indecipherable)."

"That's it then, Colin. Job done." Alice voiced.

"I don't think so, Alice. Are those guards still alive? Is there going to be proof of a crime? Lennie, who did look very sick yesterday, could go at any time. He's not going to appear in a court of law. Who, if anyone, is going to press charges?"

Alice replied, "I don't suppose those two were on your trip yesterday, love."

"I'll check Marci's list. Gosh, what an absolute gift from Len. Sorry for him, but hopefully good for us." Colin got up and paced around.

"We need Elvira to come through with something from the photo guy so we can try to get moving. Assuming she has something, she also needs permission for us to go to the burial site. But first things first; have we got the photos we need?" The two girls wandered over to the British couple.

"You look pleased with yourselves." She Lai looked quizzically at them.

"Well, so we are," responded Alice. "You tell them, love. I'm off up to the room."

Colin began, "We have had the most incredible stroke of luck. Did you see a very sick-looking bloke on the trip yesterday named Len or Lennie? Well, his daughter brought us this note. It is tantamount to being a confession and to being an accomplice to, well, read it."

He handed it over and waited impatiently.

"Well?"

"Well, yeah. What a break! We need Elvira. She's back after lunch. Hopefully, we will still be here when she gets in," said She Lai.

"You two do it. I owe Alice a bit of attention. Be good if we can all meet up for dinner tonight and make good with whatever we've got."

Over dinner, after Elvira had gotten over her delight at the news and the US team affirmed their next steps, She Lai said, "There are two photos; enhancements or not. When Elvira has them, we compare them and decide to 'go or no' with what we see.

'Go' means Elvira seeks to police and Anasazi culture support to go to the rocks and search. We must make sure we are present at any site investigation."

Colin interceded, "Alice and I are off home. The US team doesn't need help from us, and I must keep the *Bloodhounds* investigating in the UK, and most importantly, I must get Alice back to her college course." He raised his eyes.

"It is going to be difficult to get the police to accept and help us investigate. The DA approval is a prime requirement, and he is in no mood to be helpful to me," said Elvira.

"You will have to use your undoubted wares," She Lai laughed.

Pat joined her.

"She Lai will give you tips, albeit from a different standpoint."

Colin and Alice high-fived and hugged each in turn and left. As they packed, having secured a flight for the morrow, the phone rang in their room. The receptionist said that there was a caller who sounded drunk. It was Georgio.

"I wonder what he wants. It's probably more booze." Colin raised his eyebrows.

"Why did I give him my number?"

"Hello, Mr Ramirez."

"When are you coming to see me? I got information for you."

"I don't have time. We are leaving for the airport soon."

"Ugh! Are you going to Sunport? You pass real close, so call. Bring something you know I want."

"What info have you got that is important for me to go out of my way?"

"There was a guy missing from the Los Alamos trip."

Colin turned to Alice, "A brief stop off?"

"So long as we have time. Don't risk the flight."

"Okay, Georgio. If you are playing me along, I swear…"

"I'll be at the reception and wheel myself outside when you arrive at the parking lot. Stay well away from the warder!"

The couple made good time at the Rest Home, and Alice reminded Colin not to delay unnecessarily. Georgio took from Colin a brown paper bag which Georgio surreptitiously put under his wheelchair seat.

"What have you got to tell me? We have no time to spare."

"It's about Sergeant Paloma: known as Chicago Jo in my cracking days. He went back to Chicago after retiring."

He turned his chair around and laughed as he sped off to a place safe from his nursing antagonist. Colin just grinned. He then used the care home phone and spoke to Elvira on her cell phone.

"Another break! Former security guard Sergeant Paloma was missing from Marci's invitees: known at one time as Chicago Jo and said to be back in Chicago. A task for She Lai and Pat to find him, I guess."

"All our birthdays in one day!" whooped Elvira, alarming her office neighbours.

Chapter 20

It was decided Pat should chase the Chicago lead on her own. It seemed a straightforward missing person exercise, searching people lists and the like. Pat wasn't overly happy at the notion, but She Lai had an eye on likely costs. In the event, a former tennis player friend Lucy was working in Chicago and offered to put Pat up for a few days in return for a game of tennis and a decent meal.

Lucy picked up Pat at O'Hare airport and drove to an apartment on the north side of town overlooking Lincoln Park, where myriads of female footballers were playing.

"Soccer has taken over from tennis here. More's the pity," Lucy proclaimed.

She Lai, for her part, would need to use all her people skills in seeking permission from the Indian culture administration folk for access to Mel Tempi and for messing with the rocks which it was claimed had never been disturbed.

A delivery boy knocked on Elvira's door.

"Package for-" the door opened. "For you, ma'am, I guess. Gee, thanks! First of the day," as he pocketed the $5 bill with a wink.

The package contained seven large maps. There were two versions of the old monochrome photo; the original, one marginally better than the original, and another in sepia. The other two were very similar, which Elvira judged to be modern shots. She phoned the photo guy, Reuben.

"Thanks for the parcel. What's with the sepia photo? What should I be looking for?"

"Oh, I reckoned the trade to be less fuzzy than a white background."

"You could have fooled me. So what's your judgement? Definite difference, like what? Do I need a magnifier?"

"Look at my note: signed, witnessed, and dated," said Reuben.

"Thanks, Reuben. There will be no cheque in the post. We need you to retain your independence. Sorry. Bye." Elvira got She Lai on the phone.

"My office tout de suite. I've got the photos."

She Lai and Elvira lay down on the floor together to get the best view of the maps which had been laid out.

"The sepia one is better than the original. Only marginally, but better. Now to compare. Not very conclusive," murmured Elvira doubtfully.

"There are two stones or boulders near the top on the right side of the sepia picture. It says so in the note, but not so much on the newer shots."

"Yeah, I see, I see. Look!" squeaked She Lai excitedly.

"Now for the difficult bits. She Lai, Junior, and his father are due any minute, so scoot. I'll keep the parcel safe. We need to engage the DA and the police chief. Be good if you could get the Indian Culture Admin's permission for Mel Tempi access in the meantime."

"Scoot, I said," and Elvira ushered She Lai out. She Lai waited for the line to decrease and then approached the receptionist.

"Oh, you back again. What this time? Something for nothing."

She Lai inclined her pretty head, half smiling.

"No, ma'am, something for something, this time. I'll buy you coffee if you have got time and more."

"Always time for coffee. No time for bullshit; beg your pardon. I've had my share of that this morning." She put up the 'line closed' sign, and they walked off to the restaurant.

"We have the coffee; now what?"

She Lai sucked her teeth and leaned forward conspiratorially.

"We, the former DA assistant and others, have artefacts and a story which will become international news. It will feature at least on US and UK TV, soon and in a big way. The artefacts can be yours for a small non-financial price."

"Oh yeah? What artefacts and how do you know I or my chief will want them? And what story?"

"It is a shocking story and only just emerging. It has to be 'yes' now, or regret it forever. They will be queueing up nationwide to be involved, even worldwide."

"Sounds too good to be true. What price?"

"Gotcha, it's a cinch," She Lai silently cheered. She had just known that the woman had the 'I'm important' gene.

"I want Native Indian Admin permission for unrestricted access to enter Mel Tempi. This for a small group of responsible people, say six or seven?"

The guarded response from the receptionist was, "I am not agreeing at this stage. I need to persuade my chief, and you can be sure there will be no unrestricted access. The best would be guided access, an official tour."

"Okay, let's go for that for now. Can I have it in writing? I'll come back to you with a date."

"Yeah, sure."

She Lai emailed Elvira saying she had sorted the permission issue.

"Now we need the DA and police chief to join in. Over to you."

Elvira bit her bottom lip.

"I have to close my eyes, swallow my pride and not show my dislike for the DA, She Lai. It will probably be best if you are with me. You can deflect any signs of me drifting away from our objective. You will be surprised if I don't warn him of you joining us. This guy is a shit, She Lai." The latter nodded.

"I'm beginning to get that notion. Would he relish the thought of being the hero in a top scoop? That's my question."

Ray Dulatti took the after-hours call on his private line.

"What a surprise. I never expected to get a call from you, beautiful. What can you possibly want from me at this hour? Sure you can. Right now? Just bring a bottle."

He rubbed his hands, wondering. The girls made a beeline for the DA's office, knocked, and walked in.

"Oh, two of you. Who's she?"

"My assistant is on an international project, nothing to do with nuclear protesting."

Ray was downcast at not getting Elvira alone with him. He asked, "So? She's not big enough to be your protector."

"This is She Lai. She holds the aces in what I am about to tell you. Are you prepared to listen, Ray?" A slight nod of the head.

"No bottle? I will have to open mine."

Dulatti leant back in his chair, glass in hand with no offer to share, a cynical look on his face.

Elvira started, "We believe that a killing took place within your jurisdiction that you don't know about."

"What? Who? When? Where?" Ray sat upright. Election concerns were rife in him.

"Listen up, Ray, and don't judge too early. A man and a Native American woman were chased off Mel Tempi. They fled in different directions. She escaped to her village. She heard a gunshot as she fled. The man has never been seen since."

"So, no corpse, then?"

"Not yet," interceded She Lai.

"Evidence?" questioned the DA.

She Lai continued, "The woman saw two of three men and can describe them. A third accomplice has deposited what is tantamount to a confession. We are running down one of the two men seen by the woman."

"Why haven't I been told before now?"

"The killing took place over 50 years ago."

"Stop wasting my time! What evidence can you possibly have from 50 years ago? You think I'm stupid." Ray got up enraged and sloshed his wine.

She Lai held the moment.

"A pile of rocks near the Springs are said never to have been touched, but the pile changed shape from before 1942 to after 1943. This is from photos independently affirmed by an expert. We believe those rocks conceal the remains."

"Remains, after 50-odd years!" Ray's disbelief was paramount. She Lai took a deep breath, realising that this was the dodgy part.

She subconsciously twisted the ring on her finger.

"You will well know, Mr Dulatti, that there have been cases where bodies have been buried for lengthy periods and which have not decomposed, and some have."

"Most have!" Undeterred, She Lai continued.

"Scientifically, there are two soil types in New Mexico. Decomposition occurs in one and not in the other. What a coup if it should lead you to an investigation which finds evidence of human remains in Mel Tempi linking that with the names already established." She paused.

"What a potential vote winner, Ray," said Elvira smoothly, "and you don't have to show your hand until we have checked out the rocks, if at all. All is with no risk to you or your office."

"Okay. Tell me you will not go to the police chief or the Office of the Medical Investigator or anybody else. OK?"

Ray went on, "The combination of drink, you, and the conviction of your tiny friend persuade me probably against my better judgement to go along. How do we set about a look-see?"

She Lai interposed, "We need two strong guys along with you. Elvira thinks your two interns would fit nicely as well as we two and the photo expert. We will have to have a guide who will insist on coming along. The guys need to somehow secrete a pickaxe about themselves and one of those folding spades. It's easily done by wrapping it in blankets."

She Lai went on, "I'll pull things together. We should all meet at Mel Tempi and walk in together, picking up the guide once parked up. All will be sworn to secrecy." The DA's parting shot was, "I may have second thoughts. I could be putting myself on the line, so be warned."

The girls left his office. Once outside, Elvira gave She Lai a hug.

"Typical of him. Making sure we are on the back foot. He'll be there. He won't want to miss out, no matter the risk. He will always find a way of ducking any blame or criticism."

139

* * *

Pat was looking out of the plane window as the Boeing 737 was making its landing at O'Hare airport and gasped as she saw another plane on a parallel course coming in to land simultaneously.

The paunchy guy looking over her shoulder from the aisle and centre seats (he needed both) said, "Chicagoans don't do nuttin' by half, two at a time always."

Getting through security was really slow, but Lucy was waiting.

"I judged the timing right."

Hugging her friend, she said, "Let's eat en route home. No, you'll be tired. I'll phone for a pizza when we get to the apartment." Lucy stopped at the apartments' parking lot, and they went inside and up to the ninth floor on the elevator.

"Some apartment this, Lucy," said Pat.

"Part of the deal for me taking on the project for NCANCO. It's a vice-president's place. He's in Japan for the duration, so I get this apartment. The views are great; Richmond Park on one side and Hancock's tower on the other. I also get valet parking. How about that!"

Pat, impressed, said, "Wow, that's what rich folks have."

They avoided discussing business until they had eaten, swapping updates about their lives and laughing over teenage experimentation at college. Pat showed Lucy a photo of She Lai.

"What a sweetie!"

"You bet," then Pat said, "I'm looking for a man."

"After what you've just shown me, aren't we all?" grinned Lucy.

"Not me, girl! The man I'm looking for is, or was, a killer."

Lucy's head shot back.

"You what?" Pat went on to explain how she and She Lai were working as a private eye team for a Brit whose father had denied his very existence. "We know he was murdered. We just need to prove it."

"Isn't that a job for the police?"

"I find him first; if he's alive, then I hand him over to the police. If not alive, we still need to know where he was in 1943."

"Crikey Moses," Lucy expostulated. "He was alive then?"

"He went under the moniker of Chicago Jo before that. He was Sergeant Malone after he was in Los Alamos, New Mexico. Where should I start the search, Lucy?"

"City Hall downtown; voters' lists, I guess, Pat. If he was a crook, it's more like not registered, so maybe the Northside is a better bet."

"Northside?" Pat queried.

"Bad place to be: crime, drugs, police no-go area. A no-go area for you too, Pat."

The next morning, Lucy dropped Pat off in the city centre. She went into the enormous admin building. After three hours of getting nowhere, Pat gave up on City Hall and wandered into the offices of the Chicago Tribune. After being passed from pillar to post, she was eventually offered the help of an intern. He was nervous but very helpful, unearthing a 10-year-old article that included the name of Malone. A judge had been quoted as saying that more imprisonment for his latest crime was pointless at his age, and paying a fine would probably result in yet more crime. He was told not to come before the judge again.

Pat left the office and hailed a cab.

"Take me to a Northside police department, driver."

"Ninth precinct, lady, but I'll not be waiting for you. Hey, and book your return cab from inside when you leave."

Pat looked around the entrance. She thought it looked like a scary place. Deadbeats were sitting around. Cops were manhandling guys who were presumably arrested overnight. Pat shivered.

"You don't need to be in here, lady. Follow me in here and take a seat. Now, how can I help?" said the kindly sergeant.

"Chicago Jo? He left the scene years ago. He was lucky not to have ended his days in the stir."

"Was?"

"No, I think he's still with us. Quite a character, but capable of vicious acts on people who crossed him. Try the care homes. He'll be in the northside somewhere. My old buddy on the desk will know. Wait a second."

He came back shortly.

"I was wrong. His granddaughter looks after him. She is, how shall I say, a sex worker operating from home. My buddy reckons Jo babysits while she's entertaining."

Pat grinned, "Does your friend have an address, please?"

"Oh yes, he knows which apartment block, but why are you looking for Jo?"

Pat wondered how much to give away.

"It is believed he was involved in an incident over 50 years ago. Your New Mexico police colleagues will want to talk to him about evidence shortly to be notified to them by the Santa Fe District Attorney."

"Wow, sounds interesting. Fifty years ago is a bit much. We've got enough on with current cases, but glad to be of help. Let us know what happens. Where are you heading, Miss? Are you alone? You don't just walk out of here. It's too dangerous."

"Lincoln Park. My friend's apartment," Pat responded.

"Okay. I'll find you a ride. Gimme a second." He made a phone call.

"Our auto mechanic is taking a car for a test drive after repair and will put you down where you like. Safer in a marked car."

Lucy and Pat arrived at the apartment almost together.

Lucy said, "It's too cold for tennis. Too cold to venture out again. Let's call for takeout, and you can tell me how your day went."

"Good enough for me."

"The girl did good" was the response from She Lai when she and Pat shared their respective news on the phone. The whole team was flying high at the latest developments.

Chapter 21

Colin shouted to Alice. "*Bloodhounds* is on, love."

She joined him. As the programme drew to its end, Sarah gave the viewers a report back on the request put out about Catterick Garrison.

"A disappointing result, I'm afraid. Only one response with little to no information, but Gordie is going to take it up. No stone unturned; you all know the *Bloodhounds* mantra. The contact points are on the screen now, should you have use for them. Thank you and goodnight."

Gordie was on the phone almost immediately.

"Can you come with me to Richmond tomorrow, Colin? That's North Yorkshire, not Surrey and I'm telling, not asking. I'll pick you up at 10-ish."

Colin said, "Consider me told, love. You'll be back to college tomorrow, yes?"

"Oh, yes. Off first thing."

"That's okay then. I'm off to Richmond with Gordie." Gordie duly arrived on time, and Colin opened the door to him and asked,

"Fancy a coffee before we go?"

"No thanks, I've only come from Leeds this morning."

Colin shouted up to Alice, "We're off, love. I'll phone you tonight. Have a good one, love."

Gordie eagerly set off, leaving navigation to Colin.

Once on the A1, Gordie said, "This bloke in Richmond, Mike Smith, is 80-plus and nigh-on blind apparently, poor sod. His daughter,

Mary, wrote in. Seems the old boy came alive when he heard the name Jameson linked with Catterick. He does not want to be involved, but Mary thinks he should be. Thank God for pushy women, I say. Sit back and enjoy the ride, Colin."

"Has the Major made any progress?" asked Gordie as they sped along.

"Not really. The Signals museum threw up nothing. The Ministry was also a blank. Last I heard, he was trying to access regimental training records. He's either up in Catterick, or he's been and gone," Colin replied.

Gordie then asked, "What about the US?"

"Great progress. They are lining up an investigation of what we allege is the murder site and are involving the local DA. They have names. They have run down a bloke known as Chicago Jo, a right old gangster by all accounts. How about that, Gordie? We just need our trip to Richmond to produce something for the *Bloodhounds*. Be a shame not to have any progress in the UK to match up the US lot."

Mary came to the door of an old terraced house, fingers to her lips.

"Shush, Pop's having his nap. Usually only half an hour."

A voice shouted, "Who's at the door, Mary? I am not deaf as well as blind, you know." Gordie responded in kind, quick as a flash.

"It's Gordie and Colin from *Bloodhounds*, you old bugger. No offence intended."

"Mary, I said I didn't want to be bothered."

"It's not her fault Mr Smith. I can get under any unturned stone. That's why I'm a *Bloodhound*."

"Well, you'd better come in, you, cheeky sod. Gordie, is it?"

"Two of a kind, I think," said Mary. "You'll need a cup of tea."

"Yes, please," said Colin. "What do you know that might help us, Mr Smith."

"I've not heard your voice on *Bloodhounds*. Let me talk to Gordie."

"Colin is okay; just go ahead. We'll both listen." Head on one side, as if cocked, Mike began.

"I was in the Second World War. In 1942 I was called up for Signals training in Catterick. There were only soldiers there then. If you wanted out, you'd come to Richmond, four miles away. There were two athletic types in our squadron; one was a pole vaulter. He used to vault over… I don't know where he got a pole from, but he used to vault over a high fence into a compound with a food store in it."

"He'd throw stuff out to us and climb out after. A few months later, the Cook-Sergeant got court-martialled for nicking food and tecking it home up the A1 in his Austin Ruby. So we felt justice was done. Blood and thunder, I can't remember the vaulters's name. Any road up, Jimmy Jameson was the other. He was a runner."

Colin and Jordie exchanged glances.

"A distance runner, cross country, and the like. He would run the four miles and back to Richmond to buy fags and stuff for the boys. Jameson's army number was the same as mine, with one pair of numbers different. Last three 188 as against 881. You had to shout your last three, salute, and hold out your hand to get your pay, such as it were. My number was 881."

"A lot of my mates went abroad and didn't come back, and I complain about what's happened to me," Tears appeared on his cheeks.

"Enough gentlemen, I'll not have him upset," interjected Mary.
"Just-"
"No 'just' anything. Off you go, please."

Mike interjected. "No; wait; I'm all right, love. I want to say more. I may only be able to say it once, Mary. I'll do it now."

"I first set eyes on Jimmy Jameson and Frenchie at Catterick lining up for a kit. Frenchie wasn't French, but he had been living in France.

"James was a Yorkshire lad. Two good-looking fellers and both full of fun. I was lucky to have been billeted with 'em. I never heard any more of 'em after they were posted. Neither of 'em came back, I reckon. We went through training together, soldiering and technical. It's all electronics now."

Mary said, "Sorry to push you off, but his emotions come more to the fore every day that passes. It's an age thing, and I hate to see him being angry or upset." The *Bloodhounds* said their goodbyes and profusely thanked both man and daughter. Once in the car, Colin turned to Gordie.

"I hope the last three of 118 will be enough to identify my father. I should have pressed Mike for the whole number. If not, I suppose we can always ask Mary to find it and let us know."

Chapter 22

After a meeting to shape another sequence of anti-nuclear events, Elvira confided in Junior specifically to help get the Native American guide to go along with the intention to disturb the setting of what was a sensitive site for Hopi Indians.

Junior was openmouthed at the story put to him and said, "There will be hell to pay if you disturb things and don't find what you are looking for. I guess a combination of the DA and myself should be able to convince any gateman of our good intentions. It might be smart to have some cash; no, lottery tickets are better. They are not supposed to gamble and go crazy for lottery tickets."

Elvira took up the theme. "We need to convince the gateman that there is no interest in cultural aspects, just a need to reconcile a couple of photos. We will tell him we will leave with nothing. We must make it clear that we will treat the site with all due reverence."

Elvira picked up the letter of permission from the culture museum, having negotiated a wording change and naming the DA and Junior and the photo guy, Reuben, amongst the eight folks listed.

"You'll need two guides for eight visitors," was the parting shot.

The visit was set up for the following Saturday.

The DA, along with two male interns, Junior, photographer Reuben, Elvira, She Lai, and Pat, trooped into the Springs site.

"Oh, you again; this time, they did tell me you were coming," said the guardian.

"I've got my buddy with me this time, so we will be watching you."

"I am the District Attorney, and this gentleman heads up the anti-nuclear lobby for the State of New Mexico. We are both good friends of the indigenous population and respect your culture. We have too much at stake, so there is no need for special precautions."

"This permission does not say what you are here for. That, I need to know."

Reuben stepped forward.

"I am a photographer, but let me finish. I am not here to take photos. I am here to confirm that a pile of rocks is the same as it was 50 years ago. My understanding is that the pile is outside the area of special interest. That is so, isn't it?"

"I don't know about that."

"I do," said the DA.

"At least my intern does. Tell us what you found, my boy." He turned to a fit-looking 20- year-old in a light jacket and jeans.

"Right, sir. On the Los Alamos 1943 planning layout, a line encircles Mel Tempi at a one-furlong radius; that's one-eighth of a mile. Those rocks are on that line as a marker, I believe."

The gatemen seemed nonplussed. She Lai held up her hand.

"I can endorse that. I researched it at the museum."

"I don't know if I would believe her," whispered Pat to Elvira.

"So long as he does," was the riposte.

Now it was Junior's turn.

"As a token of our gratitude, I have something you might like. In my position as leader of the official anti-nuclear protest group, I am not allowed to accept gifts for fear of bribery, and these appeared on my desk yesterday."

Junior pulled out a handful of lottery tickets.

"I wondered if these would be any good to you, seeing that I can't use them?"

"Well, yes, sir. I don't think we have any such a rule," the guard replied eagerly.

"Okay, you can have them once we get to the place."

The two guardians exchanged grins.

"Thank you, sir. We'll just need to make sure you get to the line before you stop. Then we will all be happy."

"Who paid for the tickets?" Elvira asked Junior in an aside.

"Don't ask. I'll be knocking on your door when this business is over, whether the White House pays up or not. I have every confidence in you, sweetheart."

The group strode to the rocks with the interns carrying the tools hidden, wrapped in obscuring blankets. Junior turned to the guards.

"Okay, guys. Here are the tokens. Now you can leave us to our examination. We will leave the rocks as they should be left," not saying what that would be.

The group waited as the guardians left. First, Reuben took a picture of the rocks and then pulled out the photos from the A1 wallet he carried.

"Exactly as I thought," said She Lai looking over his shoulder.

"Two big boulders on the right replaced with some smaller ones. The big ones were too big to lift back up to where they were. They were able to roll them off but not lift them back up."

She Lai almost danced with glee.

The two young guys started to remove the boulders to one side.

"Only use the shovels when you must. At first sight or feel of anything, stop," said the DA, suddenly in charge and continuing, "just in case it turns out to be a crime scene."

She Lai hovered, quivering with excitement.

"That's those stones removed. Now the rest. Then the sand – whoa, easy, now," twisting the ring around her finger in agitation. The boys paused for breath.

"About three feet square; Jay Jay must have been in a crouch position," She Lai said, and standing up, added, "Looks like decomposition, more's the pity."

The interns continued with shovels.

"Looks like we are wasting our time," intoned the DA looking at his watch.

Chapter 23

Pat wasn't giving up. Kneeling in the hole they had made, she scraped with her gloved fingers. She pushed sand out of the way and exposed a piece of what looked like metal encrusted with sand; it was no bigger than three fingers.

"What's this?"

"Enough!" called out the DA. "It's a police investigation site from here on. Leave things as they are. I'll get on to the police chief. You two, stand guard until the police arrive. Don't answer any questions; refer them to me. Okay?"

"Yes, sir," the interns chorused.

Later, at the DA's office, She Lai phoned Turquoise and told her that they had been out to the rocks beyond the west side of Mel Tempi.

She said, "The DA was with us, and we had permission to visit. It turns out that the rocks mark the limit of the site of cultural interest. Before I say more, we have one last question, honey. Are you up for it?"

"Depends what the question is. I am not over the last time yet, and my daughters don't want me upset anymore."

"One single question, honestly, hon." She paused.

"Did Jay Jay have anything made of metal on him on that fateful day, possibly silver?"

"He had an army-issue pocket knife that folded. That's all. He kept it in a shoulder pack he had on when running. He said he used it to get stones out of his running shoe soles." Turquoise followed with, "Did he have something he was very proud of? Like a fastener in the shape of a snake on his Signals blue and green canvas belt?"

"It might have been silver, I suppose. Something he won as a boy. I don't know, really. Is that it, She Lai? I need my afternoon sleep. It's funny; if I sleep during the day, I sleep better at night."

"Sleep tight, dear lady." She Lai turned to Elvira.

"A snake buckle, possibly silver on a canvas belt," She Lai announced triumphantly. Elvira said, "It probably came with Jay Jay from the UK. I'll get Colin to find out if anybody knew of it from his father's army days in the UK."

Elvira turned to the DA, "I guess it's your baby now, Ray. No doubt you will enjoy telling the President about the international incident; the unlawful killing of an allied soldier."

Ray shook his head and intoned, "We don't know that it was unlawful. That's for the police and the military to resolve. I'll be prosecuting when there is a case unless it turns out to be a purely military matter. We wait and see, I reckon."

"Sorry, I'm a little late," Elvira announced as she pushed into Santa Fe police chief Justin Capper's office in the State Capitol building. Her face had got her into the building amid cries of 'How yer doing Elvira?' and 'Good to see yer, gal.'

"Hi, Justin, Ray. Who's this?" asked Elvira.

"I'm Pete Sykowski, an independent detective assigned to this case from Florida."

"Ain't necessary," said the police chief.

"Okay, Justin. Enough. It's at my explicit request, and it's not in any way any concerns about you and your officers. It is simply to be seen to be open and transparent. For the record, the President's office has given me, as District Attorney, the nod to go ahead. Okay? Is that good enough for you, Justin?"

"Let's get on. Elvira, tell Detective Sykowski the story as you know it. It will do Justin and me no harm to hear it again. This is one big case for us and the heads of State, both here and in the UK. We all need to get the story straight."

Chapter 24

By email, Colin updated the US team on the developments in the UK and said how delighted he was with the news he'd received from the US in response.

The Major was told by Gordie about the meeting with Mike Smith and being given the last three numbers of Signalman Jameson. He was able to elicit from the Signal's records of service the first five digits of his number and hence those of JJ, supposedly. The Major told the *Bloodhounds* team that the number might not exist, but the man did. A name or a number on paper could be easily lost. A man in army boots not so, especially when captured on film.

Colin hated the *Bloodhounds'* pre-programme makeup process and realised what the females of the species like Alice go through every day. He found the combination of the makeup and the intense lighting heat stifling. The rehearsal seemed to him to go on forever.

The programme itself started with the usual carry-over from the preceding week's case, and then the show's boss announced, "Within the last 14 days, we have found the man who never was in the city that never was. We suspect that he is the father of Colin Jameson, known as JJ, who was unlawfully killed. He was buried by US military colleagues in the sand of New Mexico half a century ago. There's more; J J's very existence was hidden and subsequently denied by very senior parties on both sides of the Atlantic. Sarah will lead us through the case step by step. Over to you, Sarah."

"Thank you, Henry."

She began, "I think this is perhaps the most extensive and coldest investigation so far, and it will reach as far as the heads of State in the UK and the US. So you must keep watching! *Bloodhounds* and informal American counterparts have unearthed a 50-year-old burial site in New Mexico, revealing at least one item that the local District Attorney expects will identify as belonging to JJ. That item was confirmed as the one belonging to JJ by a contemporaneous army colleague, Mr Mike Smith of Richmond, North Yorkshire."

"Mr Smith trained with JJ in Catterick in 1942/3. He also led us to JJ's army number, which our guest *Bloodhound*, Major Jon, has pursued and who commented, "The Army can lose a name on a piece of paper, but it can't lose a man in Army boots; sensible words, for which we thank you, Major."

Sarah continued, "Colin Jameson, the son of the missing father, will now tell us of the investigation developments in the US."

Clearing his throat and struggling to get started, Colin falteringly began, "As they might say in the US, my American colleagues 'done good.' Our friends in America, four young women and an older woman, Turquoise, who had a brief affair with my father all those years ago, have together investigated and are producing, with the help of the Santa Fe district attorney, a challenge to the military."

Colin realised he was rambling. He steeled himself, calling on that inner strength he capitalised on in his judo exploits.

Gritting his teeth, he went on, "This should eventually reveal what has been the mysterious disappearance of my father. To date, his very existence has been denied." He took a sip of water.

"I was a war baby. I was always led to believe that my father, whom I had never seen, had been reported missing in Europe, presumed dead. I had only seen his wedding photos until, by chance, while visiting Los Alamos in New Mexico, I spotted him on a film from 1943. Some of you will know of the research centre set up to create the atomic bomb, the so-called Manhattan Project. This was an allied forces effort and a race against the Nazis and Japanese to develop an atomic bomb."

"Last year, my wife Alice and I were on an art trip, part of my wife's pursuit of an MA. On a visit to the Santa Fe Manhattan project museum, I saw my father in a film from 1943. So we know my father was in Santa Fe then. We have come a long way since that art trip thanks to my fellow investigators in the US and, of course, this fantastic programme, *Bloodhounds*."

"The elements of proof of murder together with the name of a suspect believed to be still alive are in American police hands."

"In parallel, *Bloodhounds* have proved the existence of JJ, the man-who-never-was. This case is now of international proportions. It is the alleged unlawful and deliberate killing of a British soldier by American military colleagues. Not accidental; not 'friendly fire.'"

Now confident enough to pause for effect, Colin continued, "and I can say the next steps are likely to involve both the US President and the UK Prime Minister."

He looked directly at the camera, pausing again.

"If you are watching, Mr Prime Minister, the *Bloodhounds* will be sniffing at your door pretty soon, sir." With that, Colin sat down and mopped his brow.

"Wow! Thank you, Colin," said Sarah, who continued, "I understand we have the identity of one of the perpetrators located in Chicago, and the police there are on his trail. We need to clinch all the aspects mentioned into a definite, agreed, and clear case for presentation to all and sundry." She paused.

"It's now time to bring this week's programme to a close. I will present my thoughts to my colleagues on the approach to be taken forward. Clearly, we need to be in concert with our American friends, and we will look to Colin to maintain the link."

Turning to the camera, Sarah announced, "That is all, so goodnight from us, the *Bloodhounds* and friends. Thank you for watching."

In the green room at the BBC, there was excited chatter over wine and nibbles.

"Speaking directly to the Prime Minister, Colin, was just great. Just what I would have done," said Henry de Vere.

"We need the case to be ready to go out in the next programme."

Gordie spoke for the first time,

"Too soon, boss. Let's be sure. Let's aim for a holding message in a week and have the choice in two weeks of reporting the international responses. If, by then, we have them. Then, we can share the challenge we will have made or are making with our audience. Wriggle room if you will, but better than apologies for missing self-imposed deadlines."

"Mm! Right on, Gordie. I stand corrected. Got that, Sarah?"

Gordie fair smirked at the praise from Caesar.

Back home the next day, Alice hugged Colin and said, "That was brilliant. You were spellbinding. A whole new career beckons."

"You think so. I know not. I'm happier behind the scenes. But, I am going to pen a letter to the PM and to make sure nobody usurps my story for their own political ends."

"Like who?"

"The Santa Fe DA. Like our MP."

Later, Colin handed a draft letter to Alice.

"What do you reckon to this? I am wondering if it might be sensible to do it through a solicitor."

Alice read aloud:

"Dear Prime Minister,

I seek from your good offices the righting of a personal wrong and more.

Having believed since World War Two in 1943 that James Jameson, my father, was missing in Europe, presumed dead, I found that he had worked on the Manhattan project. To date, this and his very existence have been denied by your Defence Ministry.

The television investigation programme, *Bloodhounds* has found that 230188 Signalman James Jameson passed through Catterick Royal Signals training in 1942 and was then posted to Los Alamos. This continues to be denied by the Army.

American friends have found similar denials by the US military in Santa Fe, suggesting possible collusion between officers of the two heads of State at the time. They also have put elements of proof of foul play against a British soldier in front of New Mexico police and medical investigators. They have identified to the police a suspect living in Chicago. I now look to your good offices to acknowledge wrongdoing by previous administrations and to see matters through to the right conclusion.

I also look to you for a public apology for the hurt done to my family and me.

Further, I intend to seek substantial compensation from the UK government in due course for the absence of my father from my life, the hurt done to my mother in her time, and the expense incurred in investigating JJ's disappearance.

Also, I intend to take advice on the liability of the US government in respect of the killing, if proven. Given the time elapsed already of over 50 years. I feel it appropriate to ask you for a rapid response now. Out of courtesy, I am copying this letter to my local MP and my solicitor, my US friends, and the BBC *Bloodhounds* programme.

Yours, etc."

"That's good, Colin, but I would just write to the PM and tell him that you are placing copies for the others in sealed envelopes for our solicitor to hand out in the event of continued denials. I also think it dilutes the case to be talking at this stage about money. Focus is the watchword, don't you think? Let's get acknowledgment of wrongdoing first."

On reflection, Colin agreed and nodded his appreciation of the contribution from Alice.

"Yes. one step at a time. You are right."

"Is Elvira doing the same with Clinton? Is she writing?" asked Alice.

"No. After all, that's gone before, the DA is to do it. I'm not sure what his motive is, but it will be something to his advantage. The guy is obnoxious, but Elvira tells me she is masterminding the content, so that should be okay. I'll send her a copy of my letter, for her eyes only, and I'll do as you say and leave out the compensation stuff. I am also concerned that the letter will fail to get past well-meaning civil servants."

"Tell them the BBC are going to show the whole story on

Bloodhounds next week, including the personal involvement of the PM. Perhaps even mark the envelope to be shown on the programme."

"Nice one, Alice. I'd better tell Henry de Vere."

"No, I should tell Sarah. Leave it to her. She knows what she's doing. That De Vere is erratic; rapid-fire response to things." Sarah responded to Colin's message.

"Right, Colin, and I'll suggest the new BBC Director General probably needs to know. Is the same happening with the President? These are big stakes."

"Oh yes, we are on the move on both sides of the Atlantic, love," chortled Colin.

Meanwhile, Pat realised she had a dilemma. Roughly, she knew the whereabouts of Chicago Jo and needed to hand over the matter to the police. The Chicago police needed to know why, and word would have to come from the New Mexico police. She phoned She Lai.

"What should I do?"

"Let me check with Elvira. It's even more complicated in that an independent detective Pete Sykowski from Florida, has been invited in. Give me a minute. I'll call you back." Within minutes Pat picked up the phone.

"It's me, Pat, She Lai. How are you, partner? Elvira is talking to Justin Capper right now to get him to talk to his opposite number in Chicago. The protocol is that your Jo Malone gets questioned by the Chicago police. If they are satisfied, there is something to be answered, and they should hand him over to Capper and fly down to Albuquerque. The investigation remains with New Mexico. Elvira is tipping off the DA on what needs to happen. Stay by your phone."

She Lai rang.

"Me again, Pat. Capper jumped at the chance to be involved. Not very often he gets off his patch, it seems. It might be a good idea to talk to the local people to pin down the address of Chicago Jo and so complete the circle. We don't want to lose our suspect by default. Can you do that, Pat?"

"I don't see why not. There's a friendly guy; a sergeant on the desk; the sort who is eager to please, even my sort. I'll give it a whirl."

Pat, dressed in less masculine garb than usual but still incorporating her preferred Easy jeans, got a cab to the precinct. The sergeant wasn't on the desk but was said to be in the building.

Eventually, he found Pat, having been tipped off by a colleague that he had a boyish-looking female visitor at the desk. He ushered her into an empty office.

"Nice to see you again. How can I help?"

"'I asked you about Jo Malone. Well, it turns out he is a suspect in an old murder case. When I say old, I mean old. The murder took place in New Mexico in 1943."

"Wait a minute. New Mexico, 1943. What kind of joke is this?" He laughed.

"What are you doing getting involved in the police business?"

"Please hear me out. My friend and I are private eyes working for-"

"I do have a job to do. We are short staffed, overworked, no time for-" The sergeant held out his open hands, but Pat was quick to respond.

"Your Chief of Police is involved. By now, he will have spoken with Justin Capper, his New Mexico opposite number. Check with your senior detectives. I will need the address your colleague referred to last time." This was said to a retreating back as the sergeant left momentarily.

"Sorry about that. It seems we are to invite Mr Malone to answer questions from our detective in the presence of the New Mexico guy, hopefully tomorrow. I am instructed to tell you that you are to go now and leave things well alone. I'll get you a taxi. Don't go outside until it arrives. Nice to meet you again. Hope it all works out. I'll get you the cab right now. Wait inside until the driver collects you."

"This is a dangerous neighbourhood to be in, lady," the driver said.

Pat told him to keep the change. There was a hint of sarcasm in his thanks. He waited until Lucy opened the door to her apartment.

"I think he expected danger money," said Pat, laughing.

Later they ate in a noisy downtown Tex Mex restaurant. Between courses, Lucy organised a flight home for Pat by phone.

Three days later, Elvira heard from Capper and relayed the message to the girls, Marci and Colin, by email.

"Charges will not be pressed. The suspect has senile dementia and is unfit to plead. By all accounts, he wanders around tunelessly singing 'South of the Border' while nodding his head vigorously and grinning at any mention of Los Alamos. The investigation will be the responsibility of the Florida detective, with a New Mexico detective as an observer. The case of unlawful killing still stands on the confession of Lennie Martin. The investigation has to establish beyond reasonable doubt what happened in a court of law."

"Detective Sykowski sent the report of his findings, endorsed by the *New Mexican Observer,* to the chiefs of police at Santa Fe, Chicago, and Florida. Those findings read:

'On the balance of probabilities, a UK soldier, Signalman Jameson, was unlawfully killed by three US security guards. The victim's remains have been identified by a unique belt buckle he was known to have worn, both prior to and after his posting to Los Alamos in 1943.

Three assailants have been identified in an unsolicited dying confession by one of them. Two are deceased, and the third is unfit to plead. I am satisfied that the incident was kept hidden. Also that the victim's existence was denied. No senior US military men at the time have survived.

I believe that the top official at the time would have been culpable. The blame needs to be apportioned and shouldered now. The President may want to confer with the Prime Minister of the UK on the sensitive issue of possible collusion in denying the unlawful killing of an allied colleague. The President may wish to consider endorsing and copying this report to the UK Prime Minister.

It is understood that the UK Prime Minister intends to appear on a UK investigative television programme to respond to findings on this incident.'

"Collusion on this occasion might not be a bad idea," was the response from Justin Capper to the amusement of his counterparts. The three endorsed the report for courier transfer to the White House.

That evening the world tuned in to *Bloodhounds*.

"Good evening, and welcome to our latest, biggest and oldest investigation. My name is Henry De Vere, the founder of *Bloodhounds*. Welcome to our guest and victim, complainant, and hero, Colin Jameson."

"Colin is the son of the man who never was in the city that never was. You will be very familiar with that by now. Later in the programme, we will welcome our Prime Minister, who will respond to our findings. We are very grateful to him for agreeing to go public with us. My name is Henry De Vere, and I leave you in the capable hands of Sarah, our kingpin, for now."

"Thank you, boss, and good evening, everyone," said Sarah.

"To recap briefly. Colin never knew his father, believing that he had been killed in 1943 in Europe during World War Two. He was to spot him by sheer good fortune in a video shown at Los Alamos when visiting the museum of the atom bomb development: the so-called Manhattan Project. This led to our investigation where, beyond all reasonable doubt, we have uncovered the unlawful killing of a UK soldier by the US military. We have shown him to be Colin's father. Three assailants have been identified; two are dead, and the third is unfit to plead. US police investigations following leads provided by *Bloodhounds* have led to charges to the US President and parallel ones to our PM. We understand that the two leaders are to have conversed, and we expect to learn more about that shortly."

Sarah paused, then said, "Colin, is there anything you would like to add?"

"Just that I expect from this evening that someone will accept responsibility for what happened; will apologise for what happened and the subsequent denials and possible collusion between States. Finally, I expect that admission of State culpability will lead to significant compensation. Thank you, Sarah."

De Vere interceded.

"Sorry, Sarah. I have just been handed a text which radically changes things for this evening. The PM has been called away on an urgent matter of Government. He regrets he has had to withdraw but has no option. He offers his sincere apology to Mr Jameson and acknowledges that substantial compensation, in concert with the US, is due to him and others."

"What a shame. I feel cheated of our moment of revelation. Ah well, that's life."

"Come on, boss." Gordie came on camera. "Nobody can deny that this is anything but a phenomenal success for the show and Colin."

"Just speculating, but the Tories are in trouble, and Labour is pressing for an election asap. No wonder the PM is… I'd better not say. Suffice it for me to suggest that if I were Colin, I would be looking for compensation before this PM is voted out of office."

The programme director, who was wearing headphones, came into shot with a hand raised.

"The US President has just made a related statement on morning TV from the White House. Shall I read it?"

"Please do."

"Paraphrasing, on the widely reported unlawful killing of a British soldier at Los Alamos in the 1940s by the American military, the President says that he personally accepts the blame on behalf of his predecessors. He is not convinced that there is proof of collusion between the UK and US military, but he proffers his sincere apology on behalf of America to Mr Jameson. Apparently, he is seeking approval to put through a six-figure compensation package directly to Colin. What the British decide to do is up to the UK." There was a ripple of applause.

"That's about it."

"How about that, Colin?"

"I'm delighted, Sarah."

"I'd press the PM to match the US offer," Gordie said again.

Colin said, "My head is reeling. All I can say to the *Bloodhounds* and friends in the UK and US is: thank you." He walked out of shot into the arms of Alice.

"Well, the programme didn't go as intended, but the outcome does look much as we wanted. This is Sarah saying thank you for watching and see you next time with yet another investigation from the *Bloodhounds* team. This next from the world of tourism; couldn't be further away from the man- who-never-was. Or could it? Tune in to find out." De Vere called out.

"JJ's existence is no longer denied, nor his demise at the hands of supposed allies. Once again, we at *Bloodhounds* have left no stone unturned in our quest for the truth, for justice, for victims of injustice. Colin sought our aid and got his just deserts as well as compensation. Goodnight to you all from me, Henry De Vere, the inventor of, you've got it, the *Bloodhounds*!"

The green room was alive as crew and guests danced with joy.

From there, Colin emailed his American friends. They, of course, knew already what had transpired and were already planning a *Quebradita*, the New Mexican modern equivalent to the hoedown.

Later back at home, Colin picked up the ringing phone.

"Surprise, surprise. Our MP. Hello. Yes, it would be a good time to get you up to speed so that you can raise with your Labour colleagues the need to press my case for compensation." Alice nodded joyfully.

"I am sure Labour will be keen, especially since the Tories are in the hot seat with the voters. Our house is full to the brim with cards and letters, not to mention emails from well-wishers. This one's a vote-winner. Knock on my door as soon as you like. Bye!"

Chapter 25

Daily Chronicle front page 16 April 1997:

'Will there be matching millions for JJ's son? Colin Jameson has yet to receive a compensation package from the US. This is widely expected to be the more generous version of £1m. In dollars, this amounts to $1.6m (full story page 6). Does the failing UK PM have time to clinch a package from the House? The polls forecast an enormous loss of seats. Rumours which abound that Hollywood is considering a script for a movie of the story have been scotched. The obvious title 'the man who never was' has already been used. No title, no movie, seems to be the mood.'

Extracts from *The Voice* 12 May 1997.

'The new Prime Minister announced in his inaugural speech to the House that his first act will be not to match the US President's compensation package to Colin Jameson. In fact, only the notion of repayment of expenses incurred is said to be appropriate. Colin is angry and has vowed not to let the issue rest. He intends to continue to pursue compensation with the help of Elvira, the former Santa Fe Assistant District Attorney.

The US investigation team of four girls has agreed to arrange to meet for a Mexican meal and a *Quebradita* each Cinco de Mayo.'

She Lai and partner Pat are planning to set up a private investigating team. Having received requests for their services following the reports of their successful search for Colin Jameson's father's murderer, they are to open an office in Santa Fe. Marci is to be the receptionist and client finder.

* * *

Elsewhere, *Balloons Galore*, an oil painting by Alice Jameson MA, sold to a benefactor for £1,000 in 2002, now hangs in the Capitol in Santa Fe, and the artist continues to paint in New Mexico colours. Her new style is bold and free, totally different from the traditional material marketed to tourists.

Colin's trip to the White House was cancelled because of rumours of the emergence of a possible sex scandal. The compensation was accordingly put on hold.

Colin was asked by the new UK Labour government to put in a claim for expenses incurred on the UK front. Payment of an undisclosed amount is thought to have been made.

The US President is not to engage with Colin. His office has asked for a statement of expenses incurred in the US.

Colin continues to fight for both governments to make good their original intentions to compensate himself and Turquoise. He may have to wait for some time.

THE END

Colin often wonders about the scream and the gunshot, which was the start of his story. It has occurred to him that he may have powers of extra sensory perception.

Printed in Great Britain
by Amazon